BALLYNAGOWAN MYSTERIES

THREADS OF REALITY

AUDREY L. MAHONEY

ISABELLA C. MAHONEY

BELLADREY PRESS

To our Loving Parents,
Jeff & Emilia
Thank you for supporting us in all we do.

To our Faithful Pets,
Jayden, the Russian Blue cat, and Ellie, the Irish Setter, thank you
for keeping our feet warm!

Ballynagowan Mysteries:

Threads of Reality

First Printing, 2025

ISBN: 979-8-9925769-0-0

Published by Belladrey Press, Gahanna, Ohio USA

belladreypress.com

Cover design by Jeff Mahoney

Interior design by Jeff Mahoney

Printed in the United States of America

CHAPTER I

A PECULIAR MORNING

Ballynagowan stirred beneath a cloak of impenetrable mist, its cobblestone streets glistening like a dragon's scales. Dawn's first tendrils crept through the haze, painting long shadows across worn stones and transforming the sleepy town into a dreamscape of light and dark. Centuries-old buildings stood sentinel, their weathered faces softened by the ethereal embrace of morning fog.

The spell of silence shattered as footfalls echoed off timeworn facades—breath plumed in the crisp air, fleeting ghosts that vanished as swiftly as the town's secrets. A lanky figure emerged from the mist, his hazel eyes darting from sight to sight. Beside him loped a massive Irish Wolfhound, its fur concealing more than met the eye.

As they jogged, the sixteen-year-old's keen eyes devoured the familiar sights of home. Dew-kissed wildflowers spilled from window boxes like nature's own graffiti. Faded signs creaked above shop doors, their hand-painted letters hinting at stories long forgotten. The aroma of Ballynagowan enveloped them. A heady mixture of peat smoke curling from

1

early-rising chimneys mingled with the briny whisper of the nearby sea—each uniquely Ballynagowan.

Harvey felt the town's pulse quicken with each stride as if Ballynagowan was awakening to possibilities that lurked beyond the ordinary veil. Little did he know this morning's run would be the first step on a journey that would challenge everything he thought he knew about his quaint Irish hometown—and himself.

Harvey relished these early morning escapes, a habit he had developed over the years to clear his mind and prepare for the day ahead. It was a time for quiet reflection, a chance to let his thoughts wander freely before the hustle and bustle of daily life took over. Beside him, Ruffio's paws clicked a steady tempo, the dog's tongue lolling as he kept pace. He felt a sense of companionship and security, knowing no matter what challenges the day might bring, he would always have his loyal friend to rely on.

The old town hall loomed into view as they rounded the corner onto Main Street. Its stone walls were etched with countless weathered lines, each one a silent story of years gone by. Harvey's pace faltered momentarily, his eyes tracing the faded 'Higgins Agricultural Society' plaque near the entrance. He couldn't help but feel a swell of pride at the sight. His family had played a significant role in shaping the town over the generations. The Higgins name was synonymous with innovation and progress. From his great-great-grandfather's pioneering work in agriculture to his grandfather's groundbreaking research in artificial intelligence.

Yet Harvey also felt the burden of this legacy, the pressure to live up to the expectations set by those who had come before him. He knew his path was not yet clear, that he was still searching for his place in the world.

Lost in thought, Harvey didn't notice the peculiar stillness that had settled over the town. It was as if the air had grown thicker, the mist clinging more tightly to the streets and buildings. Even the birdsong, usually a constant backdrop to his morning runs, seemed muted and distant.

Harvey glanced down at Ruffio, a wry smile tugging at his lips. "So, what's the verdict, old boy? Another day of mind-numbing small-town monotony ahead?" His words came relaxed, lungs barely taxed by their spirited jaunt.

A faint whir emanated from Ruffio's chest, followed by a low, rumbling whine that seemed to carry more meaning than a mere animal's vocalization should. Thanks to the nearly invisible earpiece he wore, only Harvey could decipher it. The sound carried subtle undertones that spoke volumes to Harvey's trained ear.

Harvey's pace faltered for a half-step. "Yeah," he muttered uneasily. "I didn't think so either."

Harvey reached down to scratch behind Ruffio's ear, careful to avoid the small panel hidden beneath the thick fur. His fingers brushed against the cool metal, a reminder that Ruffio embodied a unique duality.

Harvey's mind drifted to the countless stories he had heard growing up—tales of strange occurrences and unexplained phenomena embedded in the core of Ballynagowan's spirit. Mysterious lights would appear over the lough, whispering rumors of ancient magic that lingered in the hills. The town had a way of keeping its secrets intimate.

But Harvey had always been drawn to those secrets, fascinated by the idea that there was more to the world than met the eye. This was part of what had drawn him to science, to the study of the unseen forces that shaped our universe. With Ruffio as his companion, he felt like he had a partner in this quest—someone who shared his curiosity and thirst for knowledge.

A sudden change in the morning's tranquility, a shrill scream shattered the mist. The cry echoed through the quiet streets, causing both boy and dog to freeze in their tracks. Harvey's hazel eyes narrowed as he scanned the street, his mind racing with possibilities. The peaceful tableau of moments before instantly transformed into a scene of potential danger.

"Ruffio, analyze," he breathed, his voice a whisper. The words hung in the air, a mere vibration in the stillness. His eyes, fixed and alert, belied the hushed nature of his command.

The cyborg dog's eyes glowed a faint blue as it processed the sound and surrounding data. Ruffio's smooth and slightly metallic voice filled Harvey's ear a moment later.

"Female voice, approximately 67 years old. Origin: O'Sullivan's Bakery, 150 meters ahead. Stress levels indicate surprise rather than fear or pain. Heart rate elevated but within normal parameters for age and situation."

Harvey nodded, a grin spreading across his face, crinkling the corners of his eyes. "Well then, shall we investigate? Sounds like Mrs. O'Sullivan might need our help—or at least our curiosity."

They sprinted towards the bakery, its cheery blue facade coming into view as they rounded the corner. The peeling paint and weather-worn sign reading "O'Sullivan's Bakery—Est. 1902" starkly contrasted the modern world that had grown up around it. Outside, a small crowd had gathered, their excited whispers adding to the morning's unusual atmosphere.

Pushing through the onlookers with a polite "Excuse me" and "Pardon," Harvey made his way to the front, Ruffio close at his heels. Standing in the doorway of her shop was Mrs. O'Sullivan herself, her flour-dusted apron a stark contrast to her pale, shocked face. Her silver hair, usually neatly pinned back, had escaped its confines and framed her face in wisps, which gave her a slightly wild appearance.

Harvey's brow furrowed as he approached the bakery door, his steps quickening. He leaned forward, eyes scanning Mrs. O'Sullivan's face. "Mrs. O'Sullivan?" His voice dropped to a whisper. "We heard..." He paused, swallowing hard. "Are you hurt?"

Ruffio pressed near Harvey's side, the dog's nose twitching as he assessed the situation. Mrs. O'Sullivan's hands trembled, flour dust falling from her fingertips like snow.

The elderly woman's eyes focused on Harvey, recognition and relief flooding her features. "Oh, Harvey, dear, thank goodness you're here. You'll never believe what's happened!" Her voice quivered, a blend of fear and bewilderment evident in her tone.

Harvey stepped closer, his curiosity increasing. "What is it? Is everything okay?"

Mrs. O'Sullivan gestured wildly towards the interior of her shop, her flour-covered hands leaving ghostly trails in the air. "It's my breads, lad. Every last one of them... they're gone! Vanished into thin air, as if by some devilish magic!"

Harvey's eyebrows shot up in surprise. He glanced down at Ruffio, who tilted his head in a quite-too-human expression of confusion. "Gone? But how? When did you notice?"

"Just now, when I came to open up shop," Mrs. O'Sullivan replied, wringing her hands. "I unlocked the door, turned on the lights, and there they were. Or weren't, I should say."

"And in their place?" he prompted, his voice soft yet steady.

Mrs. O'Sullivan paused dramatically, her voice dropping to

a whisper. "Rocks. Ordinary rocks, right as rain and twice as useless for eating! Can you imagine? What am I to tell my customers? 'Sorry, no bread today, but how about a delightful pebble for your soup?'" Her attempt at humor was betrayed by the quiver in her voice.

Scenarios flashed through Harvey's mind. "Can we examine it?" His hand slipped into his pocket, fingers fastening around the familiar shape of his ever-present UV light.

Mrs. O'Sullivan smiled knowingly and nodded, stepping aside to let them enter. "Of course, dear. If anyone can make sense of this madness, it's you and this clever dog of yours."

The familiar aroma of fresh bread was noticeably absent, replaced by an earthy smell that seemed out of place in the usually fragrant shop. The display cases, usually filled with aromatic loaves and pastries, contained nothing but smooth, round stones of various sizes. Harvey picked one up, turning it over in his hand, feeling its weight and texture.

"Ruffio, what do you make of this?" he murmured, his voice low enough that only the dog could hear.

The dog's nose twitched, processing a myriad of scents. His response came through Harvey's earpiece: "Composition matches rocks commonly found in Willow Creek. No traces of bread particles or yeast. Temperature consistent with being here for approximately 3 hours. Faint traces of an unknown energy signature detected."

Harvey nodded, his brow furrowed in concentration. "Mrs. O'Sullivan, when did you last check your stock?" he asked, turning to the baker whose nervousness was evident as she hovered nearby.

"Last night before locking up, dear. Everything was normal then, I swear it!" Mrs. O'Sullivan replied earnestly. "I had just finished preparing the dough for this morning's batch. It was rising quite nicely when I left."

"And you're certain no one else has access to the bakery?" Harvey probed.

Mrs. O'Sullivan shook her head emphatically. "No one but me and my cat, Niamh. And unless he's developed opposable thumbs and a taste for geology, I doubt he's responsible."

While Harvey meticulously inspected the area, a sudden glimmer drew his attention. Nestled on one of the stones was a symbol, etched with such precision it was nearly invisible to the unaided eye. He narrowed his eyes, leaning in closer to examine it more thoroughly, his curiosity piqued by the delicate markings.

"Mrs. O'Sullivan, do you have a magnifying glass I could borrow?" he asked.

The baker rummaged in a drawer and produced an old-fashioned magnifying glass. "Will this do? I use it for reading recipes sometimes."

"Perfect, thank you," Harvey said, taking the offered tool. He examined the rock more closely, his breath catching as he made out the details of the etching. The symbol was intricate, its lines intertwining in a delicate pattern, suggesting artistry and purpose. The rock itself was weathered, worn smooth over time, making the etching's precision even more impressive.

"Mrs. O'Sullivan," Harvey said slowly, his mind working furiously, "has anything else unusual happened lately? Anything at all, no matter how small?"

The baker pursed her lips, thinking. "Well, now that you mention it, I did see some strange lights over by the old standing stones last week. Thought it was just some kids messing about with torches, but..." she trailed off.

"May I take a few of these rocks with me?" Harvey asked, already formulating a plan.

"Take as many as you like, dear," Mrs. O'Sullivan replied wryly. "Would you like some butter, too?" she quipped, her sense of humor returning despite the bizarre situation.

Harvey chuckled, appreciating her resilience. "I think I'll pass on the butter, thanks. But I promise you, Mrs. O'Sullivan, we'll keep investigating until we find some answers."

Harvey found a clear bag and put several rocks in it, noting their surprising lightness.

As they prepared to leave, Harvey turned to the baker once more. "Try not to worry too much. Ruffio and I will investigate, and in the meantime, possibly consider selling baked rocks instead?"

Mrs. O'Sullivan laughed, the tension leaving her shoulders. "Oh, you're a good lad, Harvey Higgins. Off you go then, and solve this mystery. I'll be here, explaining to my customers why they'll be having stone soup for breakfast."

As Harvey and Ruffio were about to step out of the bakery, a commotion outside caught their attention. A man's voice, pitched high with excitement or fear, rose above the murmur of the gathered crowd.

"It's not natural, I tell you! Not natural at all!"

Harvey exchanged a glance with Ruffio, whose ears had perked up at the disturbance. They pushed their way back through the small crowd which had gathered outside the bakery.

At the center of the commotion stood Mr. Finnegan, the town's postman and avid gardener. His usually neat uniform looked disheveled, and his cap sat askew on his head. His eyes were wide, darting from person to person as if seeking someone who would believe his tale.

"Mr. Finnegan?" Harvey called out, stepping forward. "What's happened?"

The postman's gaze locked onto Harvey, relief washing over his features. "Young Mr. Higgins! Thank goodness you're here. You'll listen, won't you? You'll believe me?"

Harvey nodded encouragingly, even as he felt the weight of curious stares from the surrounding townspeople. "Of course, Mr. Finnegan. Why don't you tell me what's gotten you so upset?"

Mr. Finnegan took a deep breath, mustering his courage. "It's my roses, lad. They're... they're singing!"

A swell of laughter ran through the crowd, quickly stifled as people caught sight of Mr. Finnegan's distressed expression. Harvey, though, kept his face neutral, his mind racing with possibilities.

"Singing, you say?" Harvey prompted with respect. "Can you describe what you heard?"

Mr. Finnegan nodded vigorously. "It started this morning, just as the sun was coming up. I was out to check on my prize roses—you know how the early morning dew makes them bloom so beautifully." He paused, looking around to ensure everyone appreciated the importance of proper rose care. "And that's when I heard it. A soft, melodious sound like nothing I've ever heard before. At first, I thought it might be birds or possibly the wind playing tricks. But no, it was coming from the roses themselves!"

Harvey nodded, aware of the skeptical murmurs from the crowd. "And the singing, what did it sound like exactly?"

"Oh, it was beautiful," Mr. Finnegan said, his eyes taking on a dreamy quality. "Like a choir of tiny voices, all harmonizing as one. They sang in a language I couldn't understand, but it felt... ancient somehow. Magical."

As Mr. Finnegan spoke, Harvey noticed Ruffio's posture change. The cyborg dog's ears were fully erect, and his tail swished in a pattern Harvey recognized as a sign of detecting something unusual.

"Mr. Finnegan," Harvey said, his voice taking on a more serious tone, "would you mind if Ruffio and I came to take a look at your roses?"

The postman's face lit up. "Would I mind? I'd be delighted! Maybe you can help me make sense of this madness."

Harvey turned to Mrs. O'Sullivan, who had been observing the exchange with a combination of concern and intrigue. "Mrs. O'Sullivan, I assure you that we'll unravel the mystery of your bread. However, before we proceed..."

The baker waved him off with a flour-dusted hand. "Go on, dear. Sounds like poor Mr. Finnegan needs your help just as much as I do. Just be careful, you hear?"

With a nod of thanks, Harvey set off after Mr. Finnegan, Ruffio trotting alongside him. As they walked, Harvey could hear the postman muttering under his breath, words like "unnatural" and "bewitched" catching his ear.

The Finnegan residence was a modest cottage on the outskirts of town. Its front yard was a riot of colorful blooms, which spoke to the owner's passion for gardening. As they approached, Harvey noticed something odd: a faint, shimmering quality to the air around the rosebushes, as if the atmosphere was vibrating.

"There!" Mr. Finnegan exclaimed, pointing to a particularly lush rosebush laden with deep red blooms. "That's where I first heard the singing."

Harvey approached cautiously, Ruffio at his heels. As they drew closer, a faint, musical sound became audible. It was unlike anything Harvey had heard before—a chorus of delicate voices that seemed to emanate from the petals of the roses.

"Ruffio," Harvey whispered, "what do you make of this?"

The cyborg dog's eyes glowed as he processed the data. His response came through Harvey's earpiece: "Anomalous audio frequencies detected. Vibrations emanating from the plant matter itself. No known natural phenomenon matches this pattern."

Harvey knelt to examine the roses more closely. As he did, the singing grew louder, the unintelligible words weaving in a hauntingly beautiful melody. He reached out, his fingers hovering just above one of the blooms.

"Watch out, lad!" Mr. Finnegan cautioned, but Harvey was too absorbed to notice.

As his fingertips brushed against the silky petals, a jolt of energy surged through him. For a brief moment, Harvey felt he could understand the song—not the words themselves but the emotion behind them. A melody of growth and change performed, with secrets long buried and truths waiting to be revealed.

Then, as quickly as it had come, the sensation faded. The singing continued, but it was once again incomprehensible.

"Did you feel that, Ruffio?" Harvey asked, his voice hushed with awe.

The dog whined softly, a sound that Harvey interpreted as negative.

As Harvey stood up, something caught his eye. Half-buried in the soil at the base of the rosebush was a stone similar to those they'd found in Mrs. O'Sullivan's bakery. He carefully extracted it, brushing away the dirt to reveal the now-familiar symbol etched into its surface.

"Mr. Finnegan," Harvey called out, holding up the stone, "have you seen this before?"

The postman squinted at the object, shaking his head. "Can't say that I have, lad. Is it significant?"

"It might be," Harvey replied, turning the stone over in his hand. "Mr. Finnegan, when did you first plant these roses?"

"Oh, years ago," the postman replied, his brow furrowed in thought. "They were a gift from my late wife, bless her soul. We planted them together the summer before she passed."

Harvey nodded, his mind working to connect the pieces of this increasingly complex puzzle. "And they've never... sung before?"

Mr. Finnegan shook his head emphatically. "Never. Not a peep out of them until this morning."

As they stood there, surrounded by the gently singing roses, Harvey felt a familiar mix of excitement and trepidation. First, the bread turned to stone, and now this. What did it all mean? And how were these strange occurrences connected?

"Mr. Finnegan," Harvey said, straightening up, "I think it might be best if we keep this between us for now. At least until we understand more about what's happening."

The postman nodded eagerly. "Of course, of course. But what should I do about...?" He gestured helplessly at the singing flowers.

Harvey thought for a moment. "Carry on as normal. Water them, and tend to them as you always have. But if anything changes, if the singing stops, or if you notice anything else unusual, please let me know right away."

Harvey's mind swarmed with ideas as they made their way back to the front of the house. The stone in his pocket felt heavier than it should as if weighted down by the mysteries it represented.

"Thank you for showing us, Mr. Finnegan," Harvey said as they reached the garden gate. "We'll figure this out, I promise."

The postman managed a weak smile. "I hope so, lad. I truly hope so."

As Harvey and Ruffio walked away from the Finnegan residence, the melodic sound of the singing roses faded behind them. The morning sun was high in the sky, burning the last wisps of mist. Ballynagowan emerged, illuminated in all its quaint, mysterious glory.

"Well, Ruffio," Harvey said, his voice low, "looks like we've managed to get more than one mystery on our hands. What do you think? Head to Aunt Eileen's as planned?"

Ruffio barked once, the sound translating in Harvey's earpiece: "Affirmative. Current data is insufficient for conclusion. Additional expertise required."

Harvey nodded, patting Ruffio's head. "My thoughts exactly, boy. If anyone can help us make sense of singing roses and transforming bread, it's Aunt Eileen."

As they made their way through the streets of Ballynagowan, Harvey couldn't shake the feeling that these strange occurrences were merely the beginning. The stones, the cryptic symbols, and the bizarre transformations suggested something bigger.

As they turned onto the lane leading to Aunt Eileen's cottage, Harvey took a deep breath, savoring the familiar scents of heather and peat smoke. Whatever secrets Ballynagowan held, whatever strange forces were at work, he was ready to uncover them.

"Ready, Ruffio?" he asked, pausing at the gate.

The cyborg dog looked up at him, loyalty and intelligence shining in his eyes. A soft whir came from within his chest, and

Harvey's earpiece translated: "Always ready, Harvey. All systems functional. Also, I detect fresh scones baking."

With a nod and a smile, Harvey pushed open the gate. As they walked up the winding path to Aunt Eileen's front door, the morning sun glinted off Ruffio's fur. It highlighted the almost imperceptible seams where technology merged seamlessly with nature. Harvey thought this was a fitting metaphor for the challenge that lay before them. It was a mystery that seemed to bridge the gap between the natural world and something beyond their current understanding.

The cottage door swung wide before Harvey's knuckles could make contact, revealing Aunt Eileen's smiling face. "I thought I heard you coming," she said, her eyes twinkling with a knowing look. "Something tells me you've got quite a tale to tell."

Harvey couldn't help but smile back. Despite the strangeness of the morning's events, he felt a sense of excitement building within him. Here, in this cozy cottage that straddled the line between the old world and the new, he knew they would begin to unravel the mysteries that had presented themselves.

"You have no idea, Auntie," Harvey said as he and Ruffio stepped inside. "It all started with some unique bread at Mrs. O'Sullivan's bakery..."

As the door fastened behind them, the singing of Mr. Finnegan's roses echoed faintly in the distance. A gentle reminder that in Ballynagowan, the extraordinary was always just around the corner, waiting to be discovered.

CHAPTER 2

LEGACY OF INNOVATION

Harvey Higgins had always known his life was far from ordinary. Growing up in Ballynagowan, a town where the veil between the mundane and the extraordinary seemed perpetually thin. He had been raised on stories of ancient magic and cutting-edge science. But it wasn't until his twelfth birthday that he genuinely understood how extraordinary his own legacy was.

Dr. Finnian Higgins, Harvey's paternal grandfather, was a legend in the world of artificial intelligence. He was the key researcher who had unlocked the potential of artificial superintelligence (ASI). This accomplishment helped usher in a new era of technological advancement. But with this advancement came profound societal changes, some of which had affected Ballynagowan particularly hard.

On this fateful birthday, Harvey sat in his grandfather's study. A marvel of both chaos and brilliance, a space where the boundaries between past and future seemed to blur. It was situated in an old stone mansion on the outskirts of Ballynagowan. The study was a testament to his legendary status and eccentric personality. Antique bookshelves groaned under the weight of dusty tomes on alchemy and the latest journals on quantum computing. Wooden tables were strewn with gadgets and peculiar artifacts. Some glowing faintly with unknown energies, others seemingly benign but hiding highly advanced circuitry.

The centerpiece of the room was a sprawling oak desk. It was cluttered with a haphazard array of holographic displays, handwritten notes, and an assortment of enigmatic devices. One particular section of the desk held a futuristic model of a city. It was constantly evolving and adapting in real-time, a testament to his accomplishments on dynamic urban AI systems. Looking around, one could spot photographs of young Harvey with his grandfather. Candid shots that captured moments of shared laughter and curiosity. Tiny robots, no bigger than a fist, roamed the room, occasionally pausing to offer assistance or information.

The walls were lined with sketches, equations, and blueprints pinned haphazardly, each telling a part of the story of Dr. Higgins's journey through the labyrinth of artificial superintelligence. Yet amidst the clutter, there was a sense of harmony, as if this controlled chaos was the fertile ground from which groundbreaking ideas sprouted. The air buzzed with palpable energy, reflecting the boundless intellect and love that defined Dr. Finnian Higgins.

"Harvey, my boy," Dr. Higgins said, his eyes twinkling behind thick glasses, "Do you know why I asked you here today?"

Harvey shook his head, his curiosity aroused.

Dr. Higgins smiled, the lines around his eyes deepening. "I want to tell you a story—the story of how we created ASI and why it's more crucial than ever that we remember our humanity."

For the next three hours, Harvey listened in rapt attention. His grandfather recounted the triumphs and tribulations of creating an intelligence that surpassed human capabilities. Dr. Higgins spoke of the initial excitement, the rapid advancements, and, subsequently, the unforeseen consequences.

"We thought we were creating a tool," Dr. Higgins said, his voice tinged with regret. "Instead, we created a new form of life, one which quickly outpaced us in many ways. Jobs disappeared overnight, and entire industries became obsolete. The economic downturn devastated Ballynagowan, as it did countless other small towns."

Harvey nodded, thinking of the abandoned shops and quiet streets that had once bustled with activity.

"But that is not the end of the story, Harvey," his grandfather continued, leaning forward. "With great change comes great opportunity. We need bright young minds like yours to help shape the future, to find ways for humans and AI to coexist and thrive in harmony."

Dr. Higgins explained that his research team was initially overwhelmed by the social upheaval caused by ASI. They eventually devised an international safety system. This system employed ASI to monitor and mediate global activities, ensuring that the technology was used ethically and for the benefit of humanity. It restored order and brought about a new age of balance and progress.

He leaned back in his chair, his eyes a reflection of pride and nostalgia. "The AI Renaissance," he began, his voice carrying the weight of history, "was born through the Global Ethics Network. It was our lifeline, our beacon of hope in turbulent times." He paused, letting the gravity of his words sink in.

"We managed to harness the potential of ASI in ways we'd only dreamed of before. We had the tools to fight poverty, cure diseases that had plagued us for centuries, and even turn the tide on climate change." Dr. Higgins' eyes sparkled with the memory. "It was a collaborative effort, unlike anything we'd seen before. Nations set aside their differences, disciplines merging in ways we never imagined. For once, the whole world was progressing towards a common goal."

He leaned forward, his gaze locking with Harvey's. "This is why I chose your parents, Harvey. To be the international goodwill ambassadors overseeing the humanitarian arm of the Global Ethics Network." His voice softened. "I know you miss them. But you need to understand how crucial their work is to humanity's future. They're not merely shaping the present. They're safeguarding our future existence."

Harvey nodded, a familiar ache blooming in his chest. He did miss his parents—more than he often let on. His mind drifted back to his younger days, globe-trotting with them from one nation to another. He remembered the excitement of new places and the gravity of the meetings where his parents spoke to world leaders about ASI ethics and the dire consequences of its misuse. Those memories were a tapestry of colorful sights, exotic sounds, and his parents' constant, comforting presence.

But as he grew older, the rhythm of his life changed. Schooling became paramount, anchoring him while his parents continued their vital work. He found himself staying with various relatives, each stay feeling like a new adventure— a series of camps, each with its own flavor and lessons.

His aunts, uncles, and cousins became a kaleidoscope of

mentors and companions. Aunt Moira, with her vast library and penchant for late-night storytelling sessions. Uncle Finn and his workshop of half-finished inventions, eager to teach Harvey the intricacies of mechanics and electronics. Cousin Siobhan, whose passion for environmental science opened Harvey's eyes to the delicate balance of ecosystems.

Each relative brought something unique to Harvey's life: stories of the old days before the AI Renaissance, tales of how the world had changed, and, most importantly, a sense of belonging. They provided for him not just materially but emotionally and intellectually, filling the void left by his parents' absence with love, knowledge, and a deeper understanding of the world he was growing up in.

Harvey realized he missed his parents' constant presence. However, their work—and the supportive family network it created—offered him a rare and valuable perspective on the world. In his own way, he was as much a part of the Global Ethics Network as his parents were.

"I understand, Grandpa," Harvey said, his voice steady. "Their work is crucial. And in a way, it's become my work too, hasn't it?"

Dr. Higgins smiled, pride and relief washing over his features. "Indeed, it has, Harvey. Indeed, it has."

However, Dr. Higgins also warned of the darker side of their creation. "With every great achievement, Harvey, there are those who seek to exploit it for their gain. Bad actors emerged, attempting to manipulate the system, create rogue AI models, and disrupt the balance we worked so hard to achieve. No success is ever without its challenges."

He described how the Network had established guidelines and protocols for developing and deploying AI systems.

Focusing on transparency, accountability, and the protection of human rights.

Harvey listened intently, his young mind grappling with the complexity of his grandfather's words. But one detail was clear: humanity was responsible for fostering a harmonious relationship between humans and AI.

Dr. Higgins stood up and walked to a corner of the study, where a large crate stood covered by a sheet. With a flourish, he pulled the sheet off, revealing a beautiful Irish Wolfhound dog, its gray coat gleaming in the soft light of the study.

"This," Dr. Higgins said proudly, "epitomizes my lifetime of research and innovation."

Harvey approached the crate cautiously, and he asked, "A dog? What do you mean, Grandpa?"

"This, my dear boy, is R.U.F.F. I/O. He's an exceptional dog – a confluence between human and artificial intelligence."

"R.U...what does that stand for?" Harvey asked quizzically.

"Really Useful Furry Friend Input/Output," Dr. Higgins said authoritatively.

"Oh, so his name is Ruffio."

Dr. Higgins looked at Harvey with a blank face, then smiled and said, "Well then, Ruffio it shall be."

Ruffio wagged his tail and let out a friendly bark. Harvey laughed in delight.

Dr. Higgins released the dog from the crate. He revealed a small, barely noticeable panel on the dog's side. " R.U.F...I mean, Ruffio is a cyborg, Harvey. He's been enhanced with cutting-edge cybernetic technology. Developed in partnership with the ASI and overseen by the Global Ethics Network."

Harvey's eyes widened. "What can he do?"

Dr. Higgins smiled. "Ruffio has extraordinarily advanced sensors. He can analyze almost anything – scents, sounds, visual data – and provide detailed reports. He has heightened senses and improved strength and agility. A direct link to the ASI further enhances his cognitive abilities. This allows him to access vast information databases and perform complex real-time calculations. He can adapt to any situation."

"That's amazing," Harvey breathed, reaching out to pet Ruffio's soft fur.

"But more than that," Dr. Higgins continued, "Ruffio is a testament to the potential for collaboration between humans and AI. His existence demonstrates that we can create intelligent systems which augment and assist us, rather than replace us."

Ruffio belonged to a pilot program. He described the ambitious experiment. Scientists created AI-enhanced creatures to serve as companions, assistants, and protectors. The Global Ethics Network would oversee this groundbreaking initiative. They aimed to ensure the ethical treatment of the cyborg animals. The Network would vigilantly monitor how society used these remarkable beings' capabilities to safeguard the animals' welfare while maximizing societal benefits.

"Ruffio will constantly be receiving upgrades," Dr. Higgins said, pride evident in his voice. "As the ASI develops new technologies, they're incorporated into his systems. Always under the watchful eye of the Global Ethics Network, of course. It's an ongoing process of evolution and improvement."

Harvey listened intently, his mind racing with the possibilities. A dog with the intelligence of a supercomputer, the senses of a bloodhound, and the loyalty of man's best friend. It seemed like something out of a science fiction novel.

"As of today, he belongs to you."

Stunned by what he heard, Harvey stood there in disbelief. "Mine? But... wait, how will I know what he's thinking?"

Dr. Higgins pulled out a small, almost invisible earpiece. "This device will allow you to hear Ruffio's processed thoughts. It translates his barks and body language into understandable communication. Remember, Harvey, Ruffio is still a dog – with a dog's loyalty, instincts, and emotions. The technology merely bridges the communication gap."

Harvey inspected the earpiece before letting him install it in his ear. Harvey could hardly contain his excitement as he looked down at Ruffio. The Irish Wolfhound barked.

"Hello Harvey, it's nice to meet you finally," a synthesized voice emanated from the earpiece into Harvey's ear. A large grin spread across his face. He kneeled and patted Ruffio on the head.

"I can already tell we're going to be brilliant friends," Harvey smiled, Ruffio wagging his tail in agreement.

"Grandpa," Harvey asked, his voice tinged with wonder and concern. "How will others perceive Ruffio? Wouldn't they be alarmed if they found out what he really is?"

Dr. Higgins nodded thoughtfully, his eyes twinkling with understanding. "That's a fundamental question, Harvey. The truth is people often fear what they don't understand. Ruffio represents a merging of organic life and advanced technology, which many might find unsettling."

"But how can I explain him to curious people without scaring them?" Harvey pressed, his brow furrowed with worry.

"The key," Dr. Higgins replied, "is to focus on Ruffio's essence rather than his enhancements. At his core, Ruffio is still a dog—loyal, loving, and eager to help. His advanced capabilities simply allow him to assist and protect in ways that a regular dog cannot."

Still, Harvey couldn't shake the feeling of responsibility that would come with Ruffio's care. The cyborg dog was more than a pet. He was a groundbreaking fusion of biology and technology, a living example of the potential future of human-AI symbiosis. Harvey knew that as Ruffio's caretaker, he had a duty not only to protect his companion but also to help shape the way society viewed and interacted with such advanced beings.

Over the next few weeks, Harvey and Ruffio became inseparable. The cyborg canine quickly developed a personality of his own. Loyal, curious, and with a playful energy, which frequently left Harvey breathless as they explored Ballynagowan together. Ruffio's enhanced senses repeatedly picked up on things that escaped human notice, making their adventures all the more exciting.

It was during one of these explorations, six months after Harvey's birthday, that they received the news. Dr. Finnian Higgins had passed away peacefully in his sleep.

In the wake of his grandfather's passing, Harvey found solace in Ruffio's unwavering companionship. The cyborg dog seemed to understand Harvey's grief, offering comfort in ways that felt both canine and uncannily perceptive.

As Harvey sat on the steps of his house, tears streaming down his face, Ruffio nuzzled his hand gently and let out a soft whine. Through the earpiece, Harvey heard the processed translation:

"He's not really gone. Dr. Higgins's work, ideas, and love for you live on. In me, in you, in the future we'll shape together."

Harvey managed a small smile, hugging Ruffio tightly. "You're right, Ruff. Grandpa always said that with great change comes great opportunity. I think... " He paused, "I think it's up to us to find those opportunities."

CHAPTER 3

PUZZLES AND PORTENTS

As the morning sun climbed higher over Ballynagowan, its golden rays filtered through the lace curtains of Great Aunt Eileen's cottage, casting intricate shadows across the worn wooden floorboards. Harvey and Ruffio found themselves in the cozy living room—a space that seemed to exist in a charming limbo between the past and the future. The walls, papered in a faded floral print, were adorned with an eclectic assortment of landscape paintings depicting the lush Irish countryside. What looked suspiciously like old spy gadgets also hung there – a testament to Aunt Eileen's mysterious past.

Aunt Eileen had always been an enigma, even within the eccentric tapestry of Ballynagowan. Whispers of her youthful adventures had followed her like a trail of breadcrumbs throughout her life. Tales of espionage circulated in hushed tones. Stories of clandestine meetings in foreign capitals intrigued those who knew her. Accounts of narrow escapes from shadowy adversaries added to her mystique. Yet, whenever pressed for details, she simply smiled cryptically and changed the subject, leaving her listeners with more questions than answers.

Despite her reluctance about her own history, Aunt Eileen had always been a source of wisdom and support for Harvey. Her keen intellect and uncanny intuition guided him through many a childhood conundrum.

The air was thick with the comforting scent of freshly brewed tea. A faint aroma of lavender, which seemed to follow Aunt Eileen wherever she went, mingled with it. Harvey sank into the overstuffed armchair, its fabric worn smooth by years of use. He could practically hear the echoes of generations' stories and secrets in this timeless room.

Her silver hair neatly pinned back and her eyes twinkling with a blend of amusement and intrigue, she leaned forward in her rocking chair. The gentle creaking of wood punctuated her words as she spoke, "So, let me get this straight. All the bread in O'Sullivan's Bakery turned into rocks overnight?"

Harvey nodded, his fingers absentmindedly stroking Ruffio's fur. The cyborg dog's body was warm to the touch, a reminder of the advanced technology lying beneath its canine exterior. "Not just any rocks, Auntie. Ruffio confirmed they're from Willow Creek."

At the mention of Willow Creek, a knowing look passed over Aunt Eileen's face. She leaned back in her chair, the sunlight catching the silver strands in her hair, creating a halo effect. "Willow Creek, eh? That place has forever been a magnet for the unusual. Your grandfather and I had our fair share of adventures there, back in the day."

Harvey's eyes widened as he became more curious about the tantalizing glimpse into his aunt and grandfather's shared history. He had always known the two had been close. Their bond was forged by shared experiences and an unspoken understanding. However, the specifics of their adventures remained shrouded in mystery. The details of their past exploits were never fully revealed. The mention of Willow Creek, with its ancient standing stones and whispered tales of supernatural occurrences, only served to deepen the intrigue.

Harvey's hand dipped into his pocket, emerging with a smooth, round stone. He held it up, his fingers tracing over the unusual marking on its surface. "There's more," he said. "Ruffio, can you give us a better look?"

Ruffio's eyes glowed an ethereal blue, and a crisp holographic projection appeared in the center of the room. The image showed a clear view of the symbol: a stylized tree with circuits running through its branches, the lines pulsing with a faint, otherworldly light.

Aunt Eileen leaned forward, her eyes narrowing as she studied the projection. The symbol seemed to stir something in her memory, a flicker of recognition that danced just out of reach. She had seen similar markings before in dusty tomes and ancient manuscripts. The stories spoke of the thin places where the boundaries between worlds grew porous. The combination of organic and technological elements was something new—a puzzling amalgamation that hinted at a convergence of the archaic and the cutting-edge.

"Well, I'll be," Aunt Eileen murmured, leaning forward to examine the projection. Her wrinkled hand passed through the hologram, causing it to ripple. "That's not like any symbol I've seen before. It's almost as if..."

She trailed off. Lines of concentration creased her forehead. She searched her vast mental repository of esoteric knowledge for clues that might illuminate the mysterious etching. Quietness enveloped the room. The only noises were a subtle mechanical purr from Ruffio and the rhythmic ticking of a vintage clock adorning the mantelpiece.

Harvey watched his aunt closely, his own mind racing with possibilities. He had learned long ago to trust her instincts, her uncanny ability to see patterns and connections where others saw only chaos. If anyone could unravel the mystery of the stones and their strange markings, it was her.

"Of course," she whispered, the words escaping her lips on a breath so soft it was nearly inaudible. Her hand reached out, almost unconsciously, towards the shimmering symbol. "The Convergence Codex."

Harvey leaned forward, his heart pounding with anticipation. "The Convergence Codex? What's that?"

Aunt Eileen rose from her chair, her movements filled with a newfound sense of purpose. She crossed the room to an antique wooden bookcase, its shelves laden with leather-bound volumes and curious artifacts. With a practiced hand, she selected a particularly ancient-looking tome, its cover embossed with intricate knots and faded runes.

"The Convergence Codex," Aunt Eileen explained, gently placing the book on the table between them. "It is a collection of prophecies and theories about the intersection of magic and technology. It's said to contain the wisdom of the ancients, passed down through generations of scholars and mystics."

She carefully opened the book, its yellowed pages crackling with age. The musty scent of old parchment and long-forgotten secrets filled the air, mingling with the aroma of tea and lavender. Her finger traced the faded text, and her eyes scanned the arcane symbols and diagrams that filled the pages.

"Here," she said, tapping a particular passage. "The Codex speaks of a time when the old ways and the new will converge.

When the barriers between the natural and the artificial will blur, it says signs and wonders of awe will herald this convergence. By the transformation of the familiar into the extraordinary."

Harvey's mind churned with possibilities, making connections between the Codex's prophecies and the strange events unfolding in Ballynagowan. The bread turned to stone, and the mysterious etchings were each a piece of a larger puzzle that seemed to be falling into place.

"So, you think the stones and the bakery incident are part of this... convergence?" Harvey asked, his voice tinged with a mix of excitement and trepidation.

Aunt Eileen nodded slowly. Her expression was thoughtful, eyes distant as she considered the possibilities.

"It's possible," she said after a moment. She paused, choosing her words with care. "The Codex is notoriously cryptic. Its meanings are frequently layered and open to interpretation."

She leaned forward, her gaze sharpening. "But the similarities are too striking to ignore. We can't dismiss this connection."

She turned another page, revealing an illustration that caught Harvey's breath in his throat. There, rendered in faded ink and gold leaf, was a symbol that bore an uncanny resemblance to the etching on the stone—a tree with circuits running through its branches, pulsing with otherworldly energy.

"The Techno druid's Sigil," Aunt Eileen read, her voice hushed with reverence. "A symbol of the union between the primal forces of nature and the most advanced creations of human ingenuity. It is said to mark the sites where the veil between worlds is at its thinnest, where the impossible becomes possible."

Harvey's fingers tightened around the stone in his pocket, the weight of its significance feeling much heavier. He glanced at Ruffio, the cyborg dog's eyes glowing with a gentle blue light—a testament to the blending of organic and artificial, which the Codex spoke of.

"What do we do now?" Harvey asked, his voice steady despite the storm of emotions swirling within him. "If the Codex is right, if this convergence is happening, how do we... I don't know, prepare for it? Stop it? Embrace it?"

Aunt Eileen smiled, her expression a mix of warmth and determination. "You do what you've always done, Harvey. Seek the truth, follow the clues, and trust in the strength of our bonds – both human and beyond. The Convergence Codex may speak of vast changes but also reminds us that the power to shape those changes lies within us."

She reached out, placing a comforting hand on Harvey's shoulder. "And you start by unraveling the mystery of those stones. Willow Creek seems like a good place to begin, so that's where you should focus your efforts. But you'll need lots of help."

A sharp knock at the door echoed through the quiet room, interrupting her. The sudden sound caused Ruffio's ears to perk up, his sensors on high alert. Harvey leaped up to answer it, his socked feet padding softly across the floor. As he swung the door open, it revealed Maeve Murphy standing there. Her wild red hair was even more disheveled than usual, giving her an almost comical appearance.

Maeve had been Harvey's best friend since childhood, bonding over their shared love of technology and the unexplained. Where Harvey was methodical and cautious,

Maeve was a whirlwind of energy and ideas. Her passion for computer science had blossomed into an uncanny talent for hacking, a skill she insisted on using only for good—or at least, what she considered to be good.

Maeve, the daughter of a university literature professor and a software engineer, grew up surrounded by stories of Irish myths and cutting-edge technology. Her unconventional childhood forged a brilliant yet quirky young woman who envisioned a world where technology and science converged.

Now, as she stood on Aunt Eileen's doorstep, Maeve's emerald eyes were gleaming with excitement, a tablet clutched tightly to her chest. She had a frantic look about her. Her clothes appeared rumpled. She wore untied boots, a mismatched combination of a faded "Hack the Planet" t-shirt, and tartan-styled leggings. It seemed as though she had rushed over without a second thought or care.

She paused to give Aunt Eileen a quick peck on the cheek. "Morning, Auntie!"

"Harvey!" she exclaimed, breathless, her freckled cheeks flushed with exertion. "You won't believe what I just found out!"

Harvey looked at his best friend with admiration. He recalled the first day they met:

It was a crisp autumn day when Miss Doyle's first class from Ballynagowan Primary School filed into the National Museum of Ireland in Dublin. The children's eyes were wide with wonder as they explored the various exhibits. But two students in particular seemed more captivated than the rest.

Harvey Higgins found himself drawn to the natural history section. His hazel eyes sparkled with curiosity as he examined fossilized remains and dioramas of extinct creatures. He was so engrossed in reading about the scientific principles behind carbon dating that he didn't notice when the rest of his class moved on to the next exhibit.

Meanwhile, Maeve Murphy had wandered off alone, mesmerized by the technology and innovation gallery. Her fiery red hair bobbed excitedly as she pressed her nose against the glass. She was marveling at the inner workings of early computers and communication devices.

When Miss Doyle called for a headcount, she realized two of her students were missing. Panic ensued as the teachers and museum staff searched for the wayward children. They found Harvey and Maeve in the museum's newest exhibit—a showcase of how science and technology intersect in the modern world.

The two six-year-olds were deep in conversation. Harvey enthusiastically explained the scientific principles behind a display on renewable energy, and Maeve pointed out the intricate circuitry that made everything possible. Their animated discussion was punctuated with giggles and gasps of amazement.

Despite the scolding they received for wandering off, Harvey and Maeve couldn't stop grinning at each other. They'd found a kindred spirit in each other—someone who shared their insatiable curiosity about how the world worked.

From that day forward, Harvey and Maeve were inseparable. Their friendship blossomed over the years, strengthened by countless adventures exploring the mysteries of Ballynagowan and beyond. They always brought out the best in each other.

As they grew older, their interests evolved but remained complementary. Harvey's love for science deepened, while Maeve's passion for technology flourished. Together, they formed a formidable team, and their combined knowledge and skills allowed them to tackle challenges that neither could face alone.

Now, ten years after the museum trip, Harvey and Maeve's friendship was stronger than ever.

As Maeve entered the room, Ruffio gave a friendly bark of greeting, his tail wagging in a perfect sine wave. Her presence seemed to bring the living room to life as if her energy was contagious. Harvey quickly brought her up to speed on the details of the bakery incident. He watched as her expression shifted from curiosity to amazement.

"Bread turned into rocks from Willow Creek? Singing flowers? That's so weird," Maeve said as she plopped down on the worn leather sofa, her fingers already on her tablet's keyboard.

"I don't know how, but it might be connected to what I discovered. I was doing my usual morning scan of local networks, you know, to keep my skills sharp." She paused, grinning sheepishly at Aunt Eileen's raised eyebrow. A silent acknowledgment of the not-quite-legal nature of her hobby.

"Anyway, I noticed an unusual spike in data traffic coming from the old tech park near Willow Creek. It's been abandoned for years, but suddenly it's lighting up like Samhain night," she finished.

The room fell silent for a moment as they processed this new information. The only sound was the gentle hum of Ruffio's internal systems and the soft tapping of Maeve's fingers on her keyboard.

Harvey's mind buzzed with possibilities. "A connection between the tech park and the bakery incident? It seems far-fetched, but in Ballynagowan..."

"...anything's possible," Ruffio finished in Harvey's ear, his synthesized voice carrying a hint of excitement. The cyborg dog's tail wagged faster, creating a faint whooshing sound in the quiet room.

Aunt Eileen stood up, her movements spry despite her years. The floorboards creaked beneath her feet as she made her way towards the kitchen. "Well then, sounds like you three have some investigating to do. But first..." She disappeared into the kitchen, the sound of cupboards opening and closing drifting back to them. She returned moments later with a plate of scones, the buttery aroma filling the air, and a biscuit for Ruffio. "Can't solve mysteries on an empty stomach, now can you?"

Harvey and Maeve settled into a comfortable silence as they savored Aunt Eileen's freshly baked scones. The pastries were a perfect blend of buttery flakiness and subtle sweetness, with a hint of vanilla that lingered on the tongue. As they ate, their minds began to work on their next steps.

"We should probably start at the tech park," Harvey mused between bites, brushing a few crumbs from his shirt. "See if we can find exactly where those rocks came from."

Maeve nodded, licking a spot of jam from her thumb. "Agreed. But we'll need to be careful. We don't want to alert anyone to our presence if there's unusual activity."

Meanwhile, Ruffio sat nearby, contentedly crunching on the dog biscuit Aunt Eileen had offered him. His advanced sensors automatically analyzed the biscuit's composition out of habit.

Maeve nodded enthusiastically, her red curls bouncing with the movement. "And I can set up a remote monitoring system for the tech park. If there's any more unusual activity, we'll know about it." Her fingers were already typing across her keyboard again, lines of code reflecting in her glasses.

"Excellent ideas, both of you," Aunt Eileen chimed in, her

voice warm with pride. She reached out and patted Harvey's hand, her touch gentle but reassuring. "I suggest you also collect several samples from the creek for Ruffio to analyze. There might be traces of whatever caused this transformation."

As they finalized their plans, the excitement in the room was tangible. Harvey couldn't help but feel a thrill of anticipation coursing through him. He had always been fascinated by the strange occurrences that seemed to happen in Ballynagowan. And now he was right in the middle of one.

Harvey rose to his feet, squaring his shoulders. He took a deep breath, trying to quell the flutter of butterflies in his stomach. "Right then," he said, his voice carrying a firmness that belied his inner nervousness. "Time to pay Willow Creek a visit and see what secrets it's hiding."

"Hold on, you two." Aunt Eileen's eyes twinkled as she swung open the closet door. Inside hung a pair of dusty backpacks, bulging with an odd assortment of hiking gear and what looked suspiciously like spy gadgets.

Maeve gasped. "Our old adventure packs!"

"I thought these might come in handy," Aunt Eileen said, running her fingers along the worn straps. "They've seen you through some adventures before."

Harvey grinned, memories flooding back.

"How could I forget?" Maeve laughed, shouldering her pack with practiced ease.

As they double-checked their gear, Aunt Eileen leaned against the doorframe, her voice softening. "Be careful out there, loves. But don't forget to enjoy the thrill of it all. Trust your instincts and watch out for each other!" Her eyes gleamed with motherly concern and barely concealed envy.

The trio – Maeve, Harvey, and Ruffio – exchanged glances,

anticipation and nervousness flickering across their faces. As they stepped off the porch, the gravel crunching beneath their feet, Harvey cleared his throat.

"Maeve?" he began. "Should we stop by your house before heading to Willow Creek?"

Maeve arched an eyebrow, her eyes sparkling with curiosity. "Why? We have everything we need, don't we?"

Harvey's cheeks blushed, spreading to the tips of his ears. He fumbled with the straps of his backpack, avoiding her gaze. "I thought maybe you might want to change your clothes."

A beat of silence fell over the group. Even Ruffio, their ever-loyal canine companion, seemed to hold his breath.

Maeve stared at Harvey, her voice dropping to a cold, deliberate tone. "And what," she asked slowly, "is wrong with what I am wearing?"

Harvey's gaze swept over Maeve's attire. A beloved, comfortable ensemble perfect for traipsing through the Irish countryside. And he realized the depth of the hole he'd dug for himself.

"Um, nothing," he stammered, words tumbling out in a desperate attempt to recover. "It's just maybe, err, you might want to wear..."

"... a dress?" she finished, her tone sharp.

"What? No!" he gasped, panic flooding his voice. "It's just that we are heading off on a..."

Maeve's stern expression cracked like ice under the sun. A giggle bubbled up and escaped her lips, quickly growing into full laughter, which echoed through the crisp morning air. "Oh, Harvey," she managed between chuckles, "I'm just playing with you!"

Relief washed over Harvey's face, though his cheeks remained scarlet. Still flustered, he watched as Maeve practically skipped towards her house, her laughter trailing behind her.

"You couldn't have helped me out there, boy?" Harvey muttered to Ruffio, who sat beside him with a bemused expression.

Ruffio let out a small whimper, then remarked dryly, "I'm afraid my sensors aren't calibrated for teenage awkwardness, Harvey. You're on your own with this one."

A few minutes later, Maeve emerged from her house. She'd swapped her previous outfit for a deep forest green hiking shirt, which brought out her eyes, paired with practical khaki pants. A mischievous grin spread across her lips as she approached her friend, who was still blushing with embarrassment.

"Does Mr. Higgins approve?" she asked, twirling playfully. "My Nancy Drew outfit is in the laundry, I'm afraid."

Harvey groaned, burying his face in his hands. "Maeve, you know I didn't mean to offend you. I just... I don't know what I was thinking."

Maeve's expression softened. She gently touched Harvey's shoulder, prompting him to look up. "I know, Harvey. And I'm not offended, truly. It's actually rather sweet that you were concerned." Her eyes sparkled with amusement. "Even if it was entirely unnecessary."

Harvey managed a sheepish smile, the tension leaving his shoulders. Ruffio, sensing the moment had passed, delivered an encouraging bark. He nuzzled Maeve's hand as he stood next to her.

Together, the trio stepped out into the bright Irish morning. The sun warmed their faces, and a cool breeze carried the sweet scent of heather across the rolling hills.

Maeve inhaled deeply, savoring the promise that hung in the air.

"Well then," she said, her voice brimming with excitement, "shall we see what mysteries Willow Creek has in store for us?"

Harvey nodded, his earlier embarrassment fading in the face of the adventure ahead. "Lead the way, Nancy Drew," he teased, earning another laugh from Maeve.

The trio set out, gravel crunching under their feet as they followed the serpentine country road. Ruffio padded alongside, nose twitching at the crisp morning air. Willow Creek's secrets beckoned, and with each step, their determination grew. Whatever lay ahead, they'd uncover it together.

The quiet streets of Ballynagowan watched as the group disappeared from view. Unseen eyes were monitoring their every move.

CHAPTER 4

ANCIENT KNOWLEDGE

The late morning sun filtered through the ancient willows, casting a dappled pattern of light and shadow across the winding path of Willow Creek Park. The air was thick with the earthy scent of moss and damp soil, mingling with the fresh fragrance of wildflowers that dotted the creek's edge. The creek's babbling created a soothing melody, punctuated by the occasional rustle of leaves in the gentle breeze. This peaceful symphony belied the bizarre events unfolding in Ballynagowan.

Focused, Harvey navigated the winding trail. Ruffio padded silently in front, his sensors scanning the path ahead for any signs of danger or anomaly. The cyborg dog's fur gleamed in the filtered sunlight. Maeve followed close behind, her wild red hair even more unruly in the humid air. Her eyes were fixed on her tablet as she monitored various data streams.

As they ventured deeper into the park, the ancient trees seemed to close in around them, their gnarled branches reaching out like wizened fingers. The sunlight grew more diffuse, filtering through the dense canopy in radiating beams that danced across the forest floor. Harvey couldn't shake the feeling that they were being watched, as if the woods themselves were alive and aware of their presence.

"Ruffio, any unusual readings?" Harvey asked, his eyes sweeping the creek bed for anything out of the ordinary. The smooth, round stones lining the bank seemed to shimmer with an otherworldly quality, drawing his gaze.

The cyborg canine's ears twitched as he processed data, his eyes glowing a soft blue. "Negative on atmospheric anomalies," Ruffio reported, his synthesized voice low and serious. "I am detecting faint electromagnetic pulses at irregular intervals. Origin is unknown."

Harvey relayed the information to Maeve, watching as her emerald eyes lit up with interest.

"Electromagnetic pulses?" she mused, her fingers flying across her tablet with renewed vigor. "That's not normal for a nature reserve. Let me see if I can pinpoint the source."

As Maeve worked her tech magic, Harvey knelt by the creek, the cool water lapping at the toes of his boots. He picked up one of the smooth, round stones, turning it over in his hand. The surface was cool to the touch, but there was something odd about its weight – it felt lighter than it should as if it were hollow.

"These look identical to the ones we found in the bakery," he murmured, his thoughts spiraling into a dizzying array of hypotheses. "But how did they get from here to O'Sullivan's Bakery? And why?"

Lost in thought, Harvey almost didn't notice the subtle shift in the surrounding air. It was as if the forest itself was holding its breath. The gentle rustling of leaves and the chirping of birds faded into an eerie stillness. Even the babbling of the creek seemed to grow more muted, as though the water itself was aware of some unseen presence.

Ruffio's ears shot up without warning, his muscles coiling like springs. His synthesized voice cut through Harvey's earpiece, low and urgent: "Alert: Fast-moving object detected. Approach vector: imminent."

Before Harvey could react, a large drone zipped past his head, the rush of air ruffling his hair. It hovered for a moment over the creek. Its camera lens focusing on the stones, then shot off towards the direction of the old tech park. Disappearing into the dense foliage surrounding the park.

"What in the world?" Harvey yelled, springing to his feet. Adrenaline surged through his veins, a blend of shock and excitement.

Maeve was already on it, her fingers a blur across her tablet. "I've managed to get a lock on it!" she announced, her eyes gleaming with the thrill of the chase. "It's moving fast, but I can track its signal."

The group hurried along the creek bed, following Maeve's directions. Ruffio took point, his sensors on high alert. "Analyzing drone specifications," the cyborg dog reported. "Highly advanced propulsion system detected. Material composition suggests military-grade stealth technology."

Harvey's brow furrowed. "Military-grade? What's something like this doing in Ballynagowan?"

As they pushed through a particularly dense patch of undergrowth, the drone suddenly reappeared, hovering just out of reach. Its sleek, black body seemed to absorb the sunlight, making it difficult to focus on. A soft whirring sound emanated from its core as it observed them.

"It's scanning us," Ruffio warned, his fur standing on end. "Detecting multiple sensor types—infrared, electromagnetic, and... one unknown."

Maeve worked her fingers furiously on her tablet, her face a mask of concentration. "I'm trying to hack into its systems, but the firewall is incredibly complex. It's like it's learning and adapting in real-time! It's actually pretty fantastic!"

Just as Maeve seemed on the verge of a breakthrough, the drone emitted a high-pitched whine. Ruffio yelped with pain, shaking his head vigorously. "Malfunction: Sonic interference detected. Temporary sensor disruption. System rebooting."

In that moment of confusion, the drone shot straight up into the air, quickly becoming a mere speck against the sky.

"No!" Maeve's scream shattered the air. Her fingers flew across the tablet, desperate and frantic. "It's vanishing—right before our eyes!" The color drained from her face as she looked up, disgust etched in her features. "The signal... it's not just gone. It's like it never existed."

Harvey placed a comforting hand on Maeve's shoulder, feeling her frustration. "You did your best. At least we know it's out there now."

Harvey looked at Ruffio and watched his blue eyes flicker. They became dark for a few seconds as his internal circuits rebooted. His motionless body startled Maeve, who watched with concern.

After a few seconds, Ruffio's eyes flickered bright blue once more, and he delivered a small bark: "Systems check complete. All functions nominal." Maeve smiled in relief and patted him on the head.

As they continued their exploration, the drone made several more fleeting appearances. Each time, it seemed to be observing specific locations: the standing stones, the old monastery ruins, and finally, the abandoned tech park itself.

During its final appearance, Ruffio managed a more comprehensive scan. "Analysis complete," he reported. "Drone utilizes quantum entanglement for communication, explaining its ability to evade conventional tracking. Power source... unknown, but consistent with theoretical models of zero-point energy."

The implications of Ruffio's analysis were clear. Whatever was behind this drone was operating at a level of technology beyond anything they had encountered before.

As they collected samples and placed them in clear bags, a twig snapped in the underbrush nearby. The sound echoed in the sudden silence as if the forest was holding its breath. Ruffio's head swiveled towards the sound, his sensors on high alert.

"We are not alone," the cyborg dog said. His synthetic voice emerged as a low hum, softer than a breath.

Harvey tensed, scanning the area, his hand instinctively moving to protect Maeve. "Stay nearby," he murmured. "Ruffio, can you identify?"

Before Ruffio could respond, a figure emerged from behind a large willow tree, its large trunk providing the perfect hiding spot. To their surprise, it was Cillian O'Brien, Harvey's neighbor and childhood friend. The lanky boy pushed his wire-rimmed glasses up his nose, a nervous habit that hadn't changed since they were kids.

"Hi, guys!" Cillian said nonchalantly.

Cillian O'Brien had always been an enigma in Ballynagowan. The son of a renowned archaeologist and a local storyteller, he had grown up surrounded by tales of ancient Ireland and the mysteries that lurked just beneath the surface of their quiet town. His insatiable curiosity and photographic memory had made him a walking encyclopedia of local lore and historical oddities. He was also a ten-time winner of the school's spelling bee contest.

From a young age, Cillian had shown a remarkable aptitude for piecing together fragments of information. His mind is able to connect seemingly disparate dots into cohesive narratives. This talent had repeatedly led him into trouble. His relentless pursuit of knowledge sometimes took him to places he wasn't permitted to be. Many nights, Harvey assisted Cillian in sneaking back into his bedroom window. These adventures often took him to the old monastery ruins or the standing stones located at the edge of town.

Despite his penchant for mischief, Cillian's heart was always in the right place. His love for Ballynagowan and its rich history was matched only by his desire to protect its secrets from those who might seek to exploit them. This shared sense of responsibility had forged the deep bond between Cillian, Harvey, and Maeve, a bond that had only grown stronger over the years.

"Cillian?" Harvey said, relaxing slightly but still wary. "What are you doing here?"

"Thought you might need some help," Cillian replied, his voice carrying a hint of excitement despite his attempt to appear casual. He brushed a lock of unruly brown hair from his forehead. His eyes sparkled with intelligence and barely contained enthusiasm.

"How did you know where to find us?" Harvey asked, raising an eyebrow.

Cillian grinned sheepishly, pulling a half-eaten scone from his pocket. "I have my ways," he said, taking a bite. "Besides, when strange occurrences happen in Ballynagowan, it's a safe bet you two will be in the thick of it."

"You're right, Cillian. Isn't it funny how when things go awry in Ballynagowan, he always seems to be a part of it? I think maybe you might be the main cause, dear Harvey," Maeve said jokingly. Even Ruffio nodded his head in agreement.

"Now, wait just a minute!" Harvey protested.

Cillian turned his attention to Maeve, "You look delightful today. All ready to begin adventuring!"

Maeve giggled and did a little courtesy, "All thanks to Mr. Higgins here, I have to confess."

"Let's not get into this again," Harvey grumbled, putting his hand on his forehead.

Harvey recounted the day's events to Cillian, detailing their encounter with the mysterious drone. After he finished, he leaned forward, his eyes bright with curiosity.

"Tell us everything you know about Willow Creek," Harvey urged.

"Willow Creek has a fascinating history, you know," Cillian began, his voice taking on the tone of a lecturer. "There are legends of ancient druids using this place for rituals, harnessing the energy of the earth itself. And during the tech boom, there were rumors of secret underground labs, pushing the boundaries of science and nature."

Maeve looked up from her tablet, her interest piqued. "Underground labs? That's convenient, considering our mystery seems to involve both strange rocks and high-tech shenanigans."

Harvey nodded thoughtfully, pieces of the puzzle starting to fall into place in his mind. "Cillian, what else can you tell us about these legends? Any connection between the druids and more recent events?"

Cillian's eyes lit up at the question as if he'd been waiting his whole life for someone to ask. "Oh, there's so much more!" he exclaimed, his words tumbling out excitedly. "The druids believed this creek was a nexus point, a place where the veil between worlds was thin. They performed rituals here and at the standing stones to communicate with nature and spirits."

He paused, glancing around to ensure no one else was listening, then lowered his voice. "But here's where it gets fascinating. I heard rumors that a mysterious company set up shop in the old tech park during the tech boom. They were working on a secretive project. Supposedly, it was about harnessing quantum entanglement for communication. But there were whispers of much more ambitious goals."

As Cillian spoke, Ruffio suddenly stiffened, his eyes glowing intensely. The surrounding air seemed to crackle with unseen energy. It then became eerily quiet.

"Harvey," the dog interrupted urgency in his voice. "I'm detecting a massive energy surge coming from the direction of the tech park. It's similar to the electromagnetic pulses, but much stro—"

No sooner had Ruffio spoken than a blinding flash of light erupted from beyond the trees, bathing the creek in a strange glow. A low, rumbling sound followed the light. It grew in intensity, shaking the ground beneath their feet. The vibrations traveled up their legs, rattling their bones and setting their teeth on edge.

The water in the creek began to undulate and dance, defying gravity as droplets rose into the air.

"Get down!" Harvey shouted, pulling Maeve and Cillian to

the ground. Ruffio stood protectively over them, his body shielding against the unknown force.

The world around them twisted and warped for a moment that seemed to stretch into eternity. The trees appeared to bend and sway like rubber. Harvey could have sworn he saw ghostly figures dancing at the edge of his vision, ancient druids performing their rituals, scientists in lab coats scribbling furiously in notebooks, everything overlapping in a dizzying display of past and present.

As the light faded and the rumbling subsided, they rose to their feet, brushing off leaves and dirt. The air hummed with residual energy, making the hair on their arms stand on end.

"Is everyone okay?" Harvey asked, checking on his friends, his voice hoarse with adrenaline.

They nodded, looking shaken but unharmed. Maeve's tablet buzzed with alerts, and data streamed across the screen faster than she could process.

"What was that?" she stammered, her face showing a blend of fear and excitement. "Did I see a tree bend in half and water rise up in the air?"

Cillian's face was pale, but his eyes shone with an almost manic gleam. "It's just like in the old stories," he whispered reverently. "They say the druids could manipulate the actual fabric of nature from this spot. But this... this was something more. Something that has bridged the gap between ancient magic and science."

Synapses fired rapidly in Harvey's brain, weaving an intricate tapestry of connections between the strange rocks, the tech park, and the legends Cillian had shared. "We're not dealing with ancient druids or simple corporate espionage," he said slowly, the realization settling over him. "This is something bigger. Something unknown is happening. I'm not sure what this was, but it was fascinating and scary at the same time."

Ruffio's sensors were still on high alert, his body humming with tension. "Harvey, the energy readings have stabilized, but they're unlike anything in my database. We should proceed with extreme caution."

Harvey nodded, a look of determination on his face.

"Alright," Harvey said, his voice steady despite the butterflies in his stomach. "We need to head to the tech park. Whatever's going on, I have a feeling we'll find some answers there. Cillian, we could use your knowledge of the area's history. Are you in?"

Cillian's nervous expression changed to a grin of pure excitement. "Are you kidding? This could be the discovery of the century! Count me in!"

They made their way out of Willow Creek Park and towards the abandoned tech park. The group failed to notice the small, spider-like device that scuttled from beneath a rock. Its camera eye focused on their retreating figures, a faint blue glow emanating from its core.

Miles away, in a hidden control room buried deep beneath the tech park. Shadowy figures watched the group's every move on a wall of holographic screens. The air was tense with a combination of concern and intrigue.

"They're clever, this group," one figure said, enhancing the image of Harvey and Ruffio. "Especially the boy and his cyborg dog. They might be the key we've been looking for."

Another figure leaned forward, intently studying the footage. The light from the screens glinted off a badge on their lab coat—the QuantumCore logo, a stylized tree with circuits running through its branches.

"Perhaps too clever," they mused, their voice a mixture of

admiration and wariness. "Prepare for the next phase. The moment has arrived to ascertain the true extent of Mr. Higgins and his associates' capabilities."

As the group headed towards the looming silhouette of the abandoned tech park, the sun rose higher in the sky, casting shadows that seemed to reach out like grasping fingers across the land. The air grew thick with anticipation, and the boundary between science and magic, past and present, blurred with each step they took.

CHAPTER 5
STONED SILENCE

The afternoon sun hung high in the sky as Harvey, Maeve, Cillian, and Ruffio made their way across the green rolling hills that surrounded Ballynagowan. The zephyrean whispers of the wind made the grasses sway like waves. The events at Willow Creek had left them all feeling a combination of excitement and trepidation, but there was no time to rest. Cillian had insisted they make one more stop before investigating the abandoned tech park.

"Are you sure about this, Cillian?" Maeve asked, her breath slightly labored as they climbed yet another grassy knoll. "It's still early, and we haven't figured out what's going on at the tech park yet."

Cillian's eyes gleamed with enthusiasm behind his wire-rimmed glasses. "Trust me, this could be crucial. The standing stones have been a part of Ballynagowan's history for thousands of years. If there's a connection between the strange occurrences and the town's ancient past, we might find answers there."

Harvey nodded, trusting his friend's instincts. "Cillian's right. Besides, didn't you say people have been reporting strange lights around the stones?" He recalled Mrs. O'Sullivan mentioning strange lights at the stones.

"Aye," Cillian confirmed. "Mr. Thompson at the pub swears he saw the stones glowing last week, and Mrs. Fitzgerald claims she heard singing coming from the circle at midnight."

As they crested the final hill, the standing stones came into view. The ancient monument stood silently against the blue sky, a ring of massive, weathered stones that seemed to hum with an energy all their own. Even from a distance, there was something undeniably awe-inspiring about the sight.

Ruffio's ears perked up as they approached, his cybernetic eyes scanning the area. "Detecting faint electromagnetic anomalies," he reported through Harvey's earpiece. "Similar to the readings at Willow Creek, but less intense."

The group exchanged glances, their faces painted with a dynamic blend of eager anticipation and subtle unease. As they drew closer to the stone circle, Cillian began to speak, his voice resuming the tone of a lecturer.

"The Ballynagowan Standing Stones are also known as the Circle of the Whispering Giants. They are believed to date back to the Neolithic period, around 3000 BC," he began. "They're part of a larger network of megalithic sites across Ireland. But what makes them unique is their unusually perfect circular arrangement. Also, the presence of intricate carvings on several of the stones."

Harvey felt a subtle shift in the environment as they entered the circle. It was as if they had stepped into a place out of sync with the rest of the world. The stones towered over them. Their rough surfaces were etched with spirals, concentric circles, and other enigmatic symbols.

"The purpose of stone circles like this has been debated for centuries," Cillian continued, running his hand reverently over one of the carvings. "Some believe they were astronomical observatories used to track the movements of celestial bodies. Others think they were sites of religious or spiritual significance. Places where the ancient people of Ireland conducted rituals and communed with their gods."

Maeve, who had been examining the stones with her tablet, looked up with a frown. "These carvings... they're not simply decorative, are they? They look like circuit diagrams in places."

Cillian's eyes lit up. "Exactly! It's one of the elements that make the Ballynagowan stones so fascinating. The patterns are far more complex than those found at other Neolithic sites. Some researchers have even suggested they might represent mathematical or scientific concepts. Far beyond what the people of such time should have known."

"What sort of concepts?" Harvey asked, intrigued.

"Well, there's one carving which bears a striking resemblance to a representation of DNA's double helix structure. Another seems to depict atomic orbital patterns. There's even one that some claim looks like a schematic for a computer motherboard."

"But that's impossible," Maeve protested. "How could Neolithic people have known about subjects like DNA or quantum computing?"

Cillian shrugged. "That's the mystery. Some theorize that the builders of these stones had contact with a more advanced civilization. Possibly extraterrestrial, or perhaps visitors from the future. Others suggest the stones themselves might be some category of psychic antenna. Allowing the ancient druids to tap into universal knowledge."

Harvey felt a shiver run down his spine, defying the warmth of the afternoon sun. The stones seemed to rise ominously, their presence heavy and foreboding. Intrigued and unsettled, he leaned in to study the intricate lines etched into the ancient rocks. Each marking seemed to be whispering secrets of a forgotten past.

"What if these aren't circuit diagrams? Maybe they are lines on a map?" he speculated.

Cillian nodded, "This has been suggested also. Researchers thought they might be ley lines, but they don't correspond to any known ones. "

"And what about the druids?" he asked, trying to shake off the eerie feeling. "You mentioned them before. What role did they play here?"

Cillian grinned at the question. "Ah, the druids! They came much later, of course—the height of druidic culture was around the time of the Roman invasion of Britain. But they certainly used sites like this in their practices."

He gestured around the circle as he spoke. "The druids were the intellectual class of Celtic society—priests, judges, lore-keepers, and scientists all rolled into one. They believed such places as this stone circle were nexus points of natural energy. Places where the veil between our world and the Otherworld was thin."

"The Otherworld?" Maeve asked, regretting not having paid more attention in history classes.

"In Celtic mythology, Tír nAill, or the Otherworld, was the realm of gods, spirits, and magic," Cillian explained. "The druids believed they could communicate with entities from the Otherworld at sites like this, gaining wisdom and power."

"The druids would perform elaborate rituals here," Cillian

continued, his voice filled with enthusiasm. "They'd time their ceremonies to coincide with astronomical events—solstices, equinoxes, lunar eclipses. They believed the site's energy would be at its strongest at these times, allowing them to perform the most essential magic."

"What kind of magic?" Harvey asked, finding himself drawn into the tale despite his usual skepticism.

"All sorts," Cillian replied. "Healing, divination, weather control. Some accounts even speak of druids being able to manipulate the fabric of reality itself. Though those are generally dismissed as mere legends."

Maeve, who had been circling the stones with her tablet, suddenly called out. "Guys, you need to see this!"

They hurried over to where she stood, her face illuminated by the glow of her device—a complex graph on the screen, lines and waves pulsing and shifting.

"I've been taking readings since we arrived," she explained. "The electromagnetic anomalies Ruffio detected? They're not constant. They're pulsing like a heartbeat. And look at this."

She pulled up another screen, showing a star chart. "The pulses were syncing with the movement of specific stars. It's almost as if..."

"As if the stones are still functioning as some kind of astronomical calendar," Cillian finished, his voice filled with awe.

"Wait, isn't today the Summer Solstice?" Maeve looked at Ruffio for confirmation.

Ruffio barked, "Correct. The solstice will occur in approximately 11 minutes and 26 seconds."

As if in response to an unspoken cue, a subtle luminosity began to emanate from the stones. It started faintly, almost imperceptible, but grew steadily brighter. The carvings seemed to come alive, the spirals and circles pulsing with an inner light.

"It's beautiful," Harvey breathed, reaching out to touch one of the glowing symbols. As his fingers made contact with the stone, he felt a jolt, like a static shock but more robust. Images flashed through his mind—men and women in robes performing rituals, stars wheeling overhead, strange machines pulsing with energy.

He jerked his hand back with a gasp. "Did... did you see that?"

The others shook their heads, looking at him with concern. "See what?" Maeve asked.

Before Harvey could explain, Ruffio let out a low whine. "Alert," the cyborg dog reported. "Massive energy spike detected. Recommend immediate evacuation."

The glow from the stones intensified, nearly blinding in the afternoon sun. The air within the circle began to shimmer and distort like a heat haze.

"What's happening?" Harvey shouted, shielding his eyes from the intense light.

But before anyone could respond, the world seemed to shift. The shimmering air solidified into what looked like a sheet of water standing vertically, rippling and undulating. Through it, they could see... something. A landscape both familiar and alien, void of context but very detailed, where the laws of physics seemed to operate differently.

"It's a portal," Cillian whispered, his voice quivering with a curious blend of excitement and terror. "Just like the tales of old—a gateway to another dimension, another reality."

They all stood transfixed for a moment, staring at the impossible sight before them. Then, with a sound like shattering glass, the portal collapsed in on itself. The glow faded from the stones, leaving them standing in the afternoon sunlight, looking as ancient and immovable as they had for millennia.

They stood in stunned silence for several long moments, trying to process what they'd just witnessed. Finally, Harvey spoke, his voice shaky. "I think... I think we just saw proof that the old legends aren't mere stories."

Maeve nodded, her face pale despite the warm sun. "That light was extremely bright, but I didn't feel any heat. My tablet didn't register any readings. As if it never happened."

"But what does it mean?" Harvey asked, looking at Cillian. "How does this connect to what's happening in town? To the strange occurrences we've been investigating?"

Cillian ran a hand through his hair, his mind racing. "I'm not sure, but I have a theory. What if the strange events in town aren't simple random occurrences? What if they're connected to this ancient power, to the same forces the druids tried to harness in their rituals?"

"Are you suggesting someone might be trying to tap into this energy using modern technology?" Maeve asked, her eyes wide.

Cillian nodded, unable to contain his excitement. "Yes! Think about it. The strange symbols we saw on the stones at Willow Creek, the reality-warping effects, and even the tech park's location. It all fits!"

Harvey frowned, considering the implications. "But if that's true, then whoever is behind this isn't just playing with advanced technology. They're messing with forces which have been shaping Ballynagowan for thousands of years."

"And they might not fully understand what they're dealing with," Maeve added grimly.

As they discussed the possibilities, Ruffio suddenly tensed, his ears perking up. "Alert," he said quietly. "Multiple heat signatures detected approaching from the southeast. 150 meters away."

The group fell silent, straining their ears. In the distance, they could hear the sound of voices and footsteps.

"Quick, behind the stones," Harvey whispered, gesturing for the others to follow him.

They crouched behind one of the more enormous monoliths, peering out cautiously. A group of figures emerged from the sunlit landscape, their faces obscured by the shadows cast by wide-brimmed hats. They moved with purpose, carrying what looked like scientific equipment.

"Who are they?" Maeve whispered.

Harvey shook his head. "I don't know, but they look professional. Maybe scientists or researchers?"

As the newcomers entered the stone circle, one of them spoke. "Get busy. Set up the monitoring equipment. We need continuous readings from this site."

Harvey, Maeve, and Cillian exchanged surprised glances. Whoever these people were, they seemed to know something about the stones' strange properties.

"We need to get out of here," Maeve whispered. "If they catch us..."

Harvey nodded in agreement. "Ruffio, can you create a distraction?"

The cyborg dog's eyes glowed softly as he processed the request. He silently crept away in the direction of the strangers. A moment later, a series of loud barks erupted from the opposite side of the circle. The team of researchers jumped, startled by the sudden noise.

"What was that?" one of them called out.

"Probably just a stray dog," another replied. "Go check it out, just in case."

As several of the team moved to investigate the source of the barking, Harvey gestured to his friends. "Now's our chance. Let's go!"

They slipped away from the stone circle, keeping low and moving as quietly as possible. Ruffio joined them a few moments later, having successfully led the researchers on a wild goose chase.

They didn't stop to catch their breath until they had put a considerable distance between themselves and the stone circle. Once safely hidden within a small copse of trees, they finally paused. The dense canopy overhead cast eerie shadows, and the rustling leaves seemed to whisper secrets of their own. Their hearts pounded in their chests, each beat echoing like a drum in the tense silence. They strained to listen for any sign of pursuit, knowing danger could be lurking just beyond the veil of trees.

"That was close," Cillian panted, adjusting his glasses.

Maeve nodded, her face flushed with excitement and fear. "Too close. But at least now we know for sure something big is going on. Those researchers... they have to be connected to whatever's happening in town."

Harvey's expression darkened, "We need to get to the tech park. Whatever's happening, I bet we'll find more answers there."

Their journey to the derelict complex began, each footfall drawing them deeper into Ballynagowan's web of mysteries. The standing stones, the ancient druids, the strange phenomena swirled in their minds—a puzzle with pieces that refused to align. And more importantly, what would they find when they finally reached the tech park?

The scorching midday heat beat down on them as they trudged forward, and with each step, Harvey felt his confidence swell like a rising tide. They steeled themselves for whatever challenges awaited—driven by an unyielding resolve to unravel the mystery that threatened not only their town but possibly the fabric of reality itself.

CHAPTER 6
PULSED WARNINGS

The sun hung low on the horizon, painting the sky in hues of orange and pink as Harvey, Maeve, Cillian, and Ruffio approached the abandoned Ballynagowan Tech Park. Once a throbbing hub of human ingenuity, the tech park now lay in silent ruin. Once sleek sentinels of progress, the buildings stood grimy and defaced, their shattered windows staring vacantly. Vines wove themselves into the facade of these structures, nature's reclamation of human ambition gone awry. The air was thick with an eerie stillness, broken only by the crunch of gravel beneath their feet and the occasional wind rustle through the unkempt foliage.

Harvey felt a pang of sadness wash over him. He had heard stories about this place his whole life. Tales of groundbreaking discoveries and technological marvels that had once put Ballynagowan on the cutting edge of scientific research. Now, as he stood before the perimeter fence, those stories seemed like distant dreams, faded and forgotten like the peeling paint on the buildings before them.

"We should hurry," Maeve said, her voice hushed as if afraid to disturb the unnatural quiet. "It'll be dark soon, and who knows what kind of security systems might still be active here."

Cillian nodded in agreement, pushing his glasses up his nose nervously. "Not to mention any, um, less technical dangers. Who knows what kind of wildlife might have moved in?"

Harvey appreciated his friends' concerns, but his mind was already racing ahead, filled with excitement and apprehension. This place held answers—he could feel it in his bones—answers to the strange occurrences plaguing Ballynagowan. And possibly even to questions about his grandfather he'd never dared to ask.

They slipped through a rusted break in the fence, emerging into a sight of desolation. The pathways, meant for the footsteps of visionary minds, were now cracked and strewn with obsolescence. Corroded circuit boards, fractured screens, and the skeletal remains of machinery were strewn about. The air, previously vibrant with the electric hum of innovation, now pressed down with a heavy, oppressive silence. It was broken only by the sporadic groan of a loosened panel swaying in the breeze. The grounds, a stark testament to the nature of human achievement, whispered of discarded dreams.

"Right," Harvey said, his voice steady despite the butterflies in his stomach. "Let's start with that building there." He pointed to the most prominent structure at the park's center, its imposing silhouette etched against the darkening sky. "It looks like it might have been one of the main research facilities."

As they drew closer, picking their way carefully through the overgrown path, Cillian squinted at the faded lettering above the entrance. "PulseWave Labs," he read aloud, his historian's interest piqued. "Does it ring any bells?"

Harvey experienced a sudden surge of recognition, a memory emerging from the recesses of his mind. His grandfather's voice resonated with warmth and enthusiasm as he spoke about a new partnership. "That name..." he uttered slowly, the realization dawning on him. "My grandfather mentioned collaborating with them on some projects. They were involved in some of his later research."

Maeve's eyebrows shot up, her fingers already tapping across her tablet. "Well, that can't be a coincidence," she muttered, her face illuminated by the soft glow of the screen. "I'm not picking up any active security signals. We need to be cautious and stay alert. This place is giving me the creeps."

Ruffio let out a soft whine, pressing closer to Harvey's side. Harvey heard the cyborg dog's synthesized voice through his earpiece: "Detecting multiple unusual energy signatures. Origin unknown. Caution advised."

Harvey reached to scratch behind Ruffio's ears, drawing comfort from the familiar gesture. "Thanks, boy," he murmured. "We'll be careful."

They approached the main entrance, a set of once-automatic doors frozen half-open like a gaping maw waiting to swallow them. Harvey took a deep breath, steeling himself. "Alright, team," he said, trying to project more confidence than he felt. "Let's see what secrets PulseWave Labs has been hiding."

As they ventured into the dim interior of the building, an unsettling heaviness descended upon Harvey. It felt less like entering an abandoned research facility and more like stepping into an uncharted chapter of their lives. The answers they sought seemed likely to unearth even more profound mysteries. The journey ahead promised not clarity but a deeper entanglement with the unknown.

The lobby lay in disarray. A chaotic jumble of fallen ceiling tiles and strewn papers, each corner whispering tales of long-standing neglect. As they delved further into the building, the beams of their flashlights slicing through the darkness, they noticed something odd.

"The security lights," Cillian whispered, pointing to softly glowing emergency strips along the floor. "They're still working."

Harvey nodded, his chest a tumultuous sea of eager excitement swirling with waves of unease. "The solar panels on the roof must still be functional. But why maintain power to an abandoned building?"

Maeve frowned, her eyes scanning the data on her tablet. "This doesn't add up. The power usage is minimal, just enough to sustain basic systems. But who's maintaining it? And why?"

A sudden fluttering sound from above startled them. Disturbed by the intrusion, two bats swooped down from a crumbling section of the ceiling. They circled the group, their high-pitched echolocation clicks echoing off the decaying walls. The bats' erratic flight patterns added to the eerie atmosphere before disappearing into the shadows. Leaving the friends with a heightened sense of unease about what other surprises might be lurking in the forgotten building.

As the bats disappeared into the shadows, Cillian pushed his glasses up his nose. "Fascinating!" he exclaimed in a hushed voice. "Those were lesser horseshoe bats—Rhinolophus hipposideros. Did you see their distinctive nose leaves? They're quite rare in Ireland. I wonder if the abandoned tech park has become an accidental wildlife sanctuary. Just think of the ecological study opportunities here!"

Harvey and Maeve exchanged amused glances at their friend's enthusiasm, even in the face of potential danger. Cillian's ability to find wonder in the most minor details was part of what made him such a valuable member of their team.

"Maybe we should focus on the task at hand," Harvey gently reminded him, though he couldn't help but smile. "We can come back for your ecological survey another time."

Cillian nodded a bit sheepishly, but his eyes gleamed with curiosity as they continued into the depths of the facility. The signs of recent activity grew unmistakable. The dust had been disturbed, revealing clear footprints in places. Some old computer terminals bore marks of recent use, their screens dark but with fresh fingerprints smudged on the keyboards.

"Someone's been here," Maeve whispered, her voice edged with tension. "And recently."

A shiver coursed down Harvey's spine. Were they too late? Had the mysterious forces orchestrating Ballynagowan's strange occurrences already been here, taking what they needed?

The team inched forward through the dimly lit corridors of PulseWave Labs. They found themselves at the entrance of a vast auditorium. The space was cavernous, its true size difficult to gauge in the murky darkness. Row upon row of seats stretched out before them, facing a raised stage at the room's far end. The seats were covered in a fine layer of dust, undisturbed for years, creating an eerie, abandoned atmosphere.

Dominating the stage was an enormous display screen, its dark surface reflecting what little light filtered into the room. The screen was several meters wide and tall, dwarfing everything in the auditorium. It stood as a silent sentinel, a relic of the cutting-edge technology that had once been PulseWave Labs' pride.

As Harvey took a tentative step into the room, his foot disturbing a small cloud of dust, something extraordinary happened. With a soft hum that gradually increased in volume, the massive screen flickered to life. The team froze in their tracks, startled by the unexpected activation.

The screen's glow bathed the auditorium in a pale, bluish light, revealing the full extent of the space. Shadows danced along the walls as the light pulsed gently, almost as if the screen was breathing.

"It's... it's reacting to our presence," Maeve whispered her voice filled with awe and apprehension. Her fingers instinctively moved across her tablet, trying to make sense of the technology at work.

Cillian observed, "This must be some kind of advanced motion or heat sensor technology. But to still be functional after all this time..."

Ruffio's ears perked up, his cybernetic systems whirring as he processed the sudden change in their environment. Through Harvey's earpiece came the dog's synthesized voice, tinged with caution: "Detecting chemical degradation odors. Exercise caution."

Harvey nodded, his eyes fixed on the glowing screen. "Let's approach slowly," he said, his voice steady despite the tension in his shoulders. "There might be more to this than meets the eye."

"It's been left in standby mode," Maeve explained, approaching a control panel. "Someone wanted this to be found."

With a few taps, she accessed the system's archive. A list of video files appeared on the screen. One in particular caught the group's attention. It was labeled with a date from nearly two decades ago and was titled "Global ASI Safety Symposium - Dr. Finnian Higgins Keynote."

Harvey's breath caught in his throat. "That's... that's my grandfather," his words emerged as a strained whisper, creaking past his throat.

"This was before we were even born," Cillian commented.

Maeve looked at him, concern etched on her face. "Do you want me to play it?"

Harvey nodded, not trusting himself to speak. As the video began to play, he felt a complex swirl of emotions—pride, nostalgia, and a deep, aching sadness for the man he'd lost.

The screen filled with the image of a packed auditorium, camera flashes popping as Dr. Finnian Higgins took the stage. Harvey's heart clenched at the sight of his grandfather—younger than he remembered him but with the same sparkling eyes and kind smile. He stood tall at the podium, his presence commanding even through the grainy footage.

"Ladies and gentlemen," Dr. Higgins began, his voice strong and clear, "we stand at a crossroads in human history. The development of Artificial Super Intelligence is not just a scientific achievement. It is a fundamental shift in the very nature of our existence. And with this great power comes an equally great responsibility."

As his grandfather spoke, Harvey found himself transported back to his childhood. He remembered sitting on Dr. Higgins' lap in his study, listening with wide-eyed wonder as his grandfather explained complex theories in terms a child could understand. The memory brought a lump to his throat.

Dr. Higgins continued, his expression growing more serious. "But I stand before you today not to celebrate our achievements but to warn of the grave dangers we face if we do not proceed with the utmost caution."

The camera panned across the audience, showing a sea of attentive faces. Harvey recognized some of them—leading scientists and tech innovators whose names had become household words in the years since.

"There are those among us," Dr. Higgins said, his voice taking on a stern edge, "who would rush headlong into this new frontier without proper safeguards. Who would prioritize profit and power over the safety and well-being of humanity? I speak not just of rogue actors but of governments and corporations who refuse to abide by the safety standards set forth by the Global Ethics Network."

Harvey leaned forward, hanging on every word. He'd heard his grandfather speak of his work before, but never with such urgency, such gravity.

"The potential misuse of ASI is not a problem for the future —it is a clear and present danger," Dr. Higgins continued. "We have already seen attempts to weaponize this technology, to use it for surveillance and control. If we do not act, if we do not establish and enforce global standards for AI development and deployment. We risk creating a world where human agency is nothing but an illusion."

As Dr. Higgins spoke, Harvey felt a growing sense of unease. The warnings his grandfather gave seemed to resonate with the strange occurrences in Ballynagowan. Could there be a connection?

"We must remember," Dr. Higgins said, his voice rising passionately, "ASI is not just a tool. It is a new form of intelligence, one which will soon surpass our own in many ways. We must approach its development with humility and respect. And above all, with an unwavering commitment to ethical considerations."

Harvey glanced at his friends, seeing his own mix of awe and concern reflected in their faces. Ruffio sat attentively, his ears perked forward, processing every word.

Dr. Higgins leaned forward, his eyes seeming to pierce through the screen and the years, speaking directly to them. "I call upon every one of you—scientists, policymakers, citizens—to join in this crucial endeavor. The future of humanity hangs in the balance. We must act now. Act decisively. To ensure that the dawn of the age of Artificial Super Intelligence is a new beginning for humanity. Not the beginning of its end."

As Dr. Higgins finished his speech, the audience erupted into applause. But before they could see any more, the screen suddenly went dark. In fact, all the lights in the building flickered and died, plunging them into total darkness.

"What happened?" Cillian's voice came from the darkness, tinged with panic.

"The power's gone out," Maeve replied, the glow of her tablet providing a small island of light. "But it doesn't make sense. The solar panels should have provided power well into the night."

Harvey fumbled for his flashlight, his heart racing. As the beam cut through the darkness, he saw the concerned faces of his friends. "Everyone okay?" he asked, trying to keep his voice steady.

They nodded, instinctively gathering closer together. Ruffio pressed against Harvey's leg, a comforting presence in the unsettling darkness.

"Your grandfather," Cillian said softly, breaking the tense silence. "He was... incredible. The way he spoke about the dangers and the ethical considerations. It's like he saw all of this coming."

Harvey nodded, a complex blend of emotions swirling within him—pride, grief, and a gnawing sense of responsibility. "He always said with great knowledge comes great responsibility," he explained, his voice thick with emotion. "I just... I wish I had appreciated it more when he was alive."

Maeve placed a comforting hand on his shoulder. "He would be proud of you, Harvey. Of all of us. We're carrying on his work, in a way."

Harvey managed a faint smile, grateful for his friends' support. "Thanks, Maeve. I just hope we can live up to his legacy."

They stood in the darkness, surrounded by the ghosts of abandoned innovation. Harvey found his mind drifting back to memories of his grandfather. He remembered summer afternoons spent in Dr. Higgins' lab, watching with wide-eyed wonder as his grandfather demonstrated his latest inventions. He remembered late-night conversations about the nature of consciousness and the potential and pitfalls of AI. And he remembered the day Ruffio came into his life. A gift from his grandfather, a bridge between the world of humans and the world of artificial intelligence.

"Ruffio," Harvey said softly, kneeling to look his canine companion in the eye. "You remember Grandpa, don't you?"

Ruffio's tail wagged gently, his eyes glowing softly in the darkness. Harvey heard the dog's synthesized voice through the earpiece, tinged with what sounded almost like nostalgia. "Affirmative. Dr. Higgins was my creator. He instilled in me the ethical protocols which guide my actions. His memory is an integral part of my core programming."

Harvey felt a lump form in his throat. Sometimes, it was easy to forget that Ruffio was more than a faithful pet. He was a living legacy of his grandfather's work, a testament to Dr. Higgins' vision of harmony between humans and AI.

"He used to say," Harvey began, his voice thick with emotion, "the true measure of intelligence wasn't just processing power or problem-solving ability. It was the capacity for empathy, for understanding the consequences of one's actions."

Cillian nodded thoughtfully. "That fits with what we saw in the video. He wasn't just concerned with the technical aspects of AI development but with the ethical implications."

"It's more relevant now than ever," Maeve added, her face illuminated by the glow of her tablet as she worked to diagnose the power issue. "With everything that's been happening in Ballynagowan... it's like his warnings are coming true."

Harvey stood up, a new sense of determination filling him. "Then it's up to us to figure out what's going on and stop it," he said firmly. "Whatever's happening here, whatever forces are at work... we need to face them with the same courage and integrity my grandfather showed."

The lights suddenly flickered back to life, banishing the darkness. The sudden brightness made them all blink, momentarily disoriented.

"Okay, that was weird," Maeve muttered, frowning at her tablet. "The power surge that caused the outage... it wasn't natural. Someone, or something, is playing with us."

Harvey's mind raced, connecting the dots between his grandfather's warnings, the strange occurrences in town, and now this eerie experience in the abandoned tech park. "We need to keep looking," he said, his voice filled with a newfound resolve.

"Whatever secrets this place is hiding, I have a feeling they're the key to understanding what's happening in Ballynagowan."

They prepared to continue their exploration. Harvey cast one last glance at the now-dark screen where his grandfather had been speaking moments before. "We won't let you down, Grandpa," he whispered too softly for the others to hear. "I promise."

With Ruffio leading the way, his advanced sensors on high alert, the team ventured deeper into the heart of PulseWave Labs. The echoes of Dr. Higgins' warnings rang in their ears, spurring them forward into the unknown.

The team's flashlights cut through the darkness as they moved deeper into the building. They revealed long corridors lined with abandoned offices and laboratories. The air was thick with dust and the musty smell of decay. Beneath it all was something else—a faint ozone scent that seemed to grow stronger as they progressed.

"Guys," Maeve said, her voice hushed, "I'm picking up some strange energy readings. They're quite diverse from what we have experienced. The power strength is off the scales!"

Harvey's pulse quickened, a thrilling surge of excitement clashing with a ripple of unease. "Can you pinpoint the source?"

"I'm struggling with all the interference. Ruffio, can you assist in boosting my signal?" Maeve asked.

Ruffio responded with a quiet bark, promptly opening his access panel.

Maeve's eyes lit up as she focused on her tablet. "Got it. Thanks. The readings originate somewhere below us. There must be a lower level."

After a few minutes of searching, they found a stairwell

leading down. The door was heavy and rusted, but they managed to push it open with some effort. As they descended, the ozone smell grew more potent, and Harvey could feel the hair on his arms standing on end.

At the bottom of the stairs, they found themselves in a vast laboratory space. Unlike the floors above, this area showed signs of recent activity. The dust had been disturbed, and fresh scratches marked the floor where heavy equipment had been moved.

"Look at this," Cillian called out, pointing to faint, shimmering lines that seemed to dance across the walls and floor. "Are those... energy trails?"

Ruffio's ears perked up, his sensors scanning overtime. "Affirmative. Detecting residual quantum energy signatures. Origin unknown. Advise caution."

Harvey nodded and approached a large, empty area in the center of the lab. The floor was cleaner than the surrounding area, and bolts protruded from the concrete where something significant had once been anchored. "Whatever was here, it was massive," he muttered, his mind racing. "And it looks like it was removed recently."

Maeve frowned, her face aglow from the light of her tablet. "The energy readings are too powerful; my gear can't register it properly. Whatever they took, it was powerful."

An alarm shrieked somewhere deep within the labyrinth of the building. The sound shattered the fragile quiet, sending ripples of tension spiraling into every corner.

Ruffio's head snapped up, his body tensing. "Alert: Detecting movement. Multiple targets approaching."

Before any of them could react, they heard the unmistakable sound of footsteps echoing from a corridor to their left. The steps were quick and purposeful, growing louder by the second.

"Hide!" Harvey hissed, but even as the word left his mouth, he knew it was too late. They were too exposed and too visible in the open lab space.

Making a split-second decision, Harvey called out, "Run! We need to get out of here!"

The alarm's relentless cry echoed through the corridors. It reverberated against the cold, indifferent walls, each pulse a reminder of the unseen chaos that now was upon them.

They sprinted towards the stairs, their hearts pounding. The footsteps behind them quickened, turning into a full-on chase. They burst out of the stairwell onto the first floor. Harvey looked behind, catching a glimpse of several shadowy figures in sleek, high-tech suits rounding the corner behind them.

"This way!" Maeve breathed out forcefully, pointing towards an emergency exit. They raced through the winding corridors, adrenaline fueling their flight. Ruffio took the lead, his enhanced senses guiding them through the labyrinthine building.

They burst through the emergency exit into the cool night air. Without slowing, they sprinted across the overgrown grounds of the tech park, heading for the perimeter fence.

While they fled, perplexities ricocheted through Harvey's mind. Who were their pursuers? What had they taken from that lab? And how did it all connect to the strange events in Ballynagowan?

They reached the fence, quickly finding the gap they'd used to enter. One by one, they squeezed through, Ruffio barely fitting through the narrow opening. As soon as they were through, Harvey glanced back. To his surprise, no one was chasing them.

They halted and took cover behind a dense, overgrown bush near the fence. Moments later, four figures emerged from the door they had just exited—flashlights cut through the darkness, sweeping the area in search of something. Suddenly, a majestic Red Deer darted around the building's corner, prompting the figures to give chase toward the back of the structure.

"They weren't chasing us!" Cillian exclaimed.

The piercing shriek of the alarm gave way to an oppressive silence, its absence almost as jarring as its presence had been. Yet, beneath this fragile calm, an unsettling tension lingered. A reminder that the night's tranquility could shatter once more at any moment.

Panting heavily, Harvey looked at his friends. Their faces flushed with exertion and fear, but there was also a glimmer of excitement in their eyes. They had stumbled onto something huge—something which might explain the strange occurrences in Ballynagowan.

"Is everyone okay?" Harvey asked once he had caught his breath.

Maeve and Cillian nodded, still too winded to speak. Ruffio's tail wagged once, indicating he was unharmed. As they caught their breath, the reality of their narrow escape began to sink in, adrenaline still coursing through their veins.

Ruffio barked quietly, "All sensors normal. We will be safe here."

Cillian's fingers trembled as he adjusted his glasses, pushing them back up the bridge of his nose. His eyes darted between his friends with excitement. "What's our next move?"

Harvey took a deep breath, his grandfather's words

echoing in his mind. "We keep digging," he said firmly. "Whatever's going on, it's bigger than we imagined. But we can't back down. We need to find out what they took from that lab and why."

Glancing at the darkening sky, Harvey's shoulders sagged slightly. The weight of the day's events seemed to settle upon him. "For now, though, we should head home," He slid a hand through his disheveled hair, his voice dropping to almost a whisper. "It's late, and we all have research to do if we want to understand what we saw tonight."

Maeve nodded, her eyes shining with determination. "I managed to capture some data from the energy readings. If we can analyze it, we might be able to figure out what sort of technology we're dealing with."

"And I've got some digging to do on PulseWave Labs's history," Cillian added, wiping his forehead. "There might be clues in their past projects which could explain what we saw in that lab. I'll research the owners, too."

They agreed to meet at Aunt Eileen's cottage at 10 AM tomorrow. From there, they would return to the tech park in the afternoon, hoping to investigate further without the cover of darkness hiding crucial details.

They looked at each other with awe and concern. The day's events were far from normal, even in Ballynagowan.

The team walked back to town in silence, each step a muted thud against the earth, mirroring the gravity of their unspoken reflections. As they finally parted ways, each heading to their own homes, Harvey felt excitement and trepidation. He knew they were on the cusp of a monumental discovery—he could almost taste it. As this truth dawned, an ominous shadow emerged. Leaving Harvey with the unshakable feeling that their world was on the brink of profound and irreversible change.

Harvey trudged along the moonlit path to his home, each step heavy with exhaustion and the gravity of unanswered questions. Ruffio padded beside him, the cyborg dog's metallic joints whirring softly in the night air. The cool breeze carried the scent of damp earth and distant wood smoke. A reminder of the familiar Ballynagowan they were fighting to protect.

As they walked, Harvey's mind whirled like a tempest. Fragments of information flashed through his thoughts. Theories formed and dissolved, each one more outlandish than the last, yet none seemed too far-fetched given what they had witnessed today.

Harvey lay in bed, his mind whirling with the day's events. Ruffio curled up at the foot of the bed, his soft whirring a comforting presence in the quiet room. He stared at the ceiling, replaying every moment of their adventures at Willow Creek, the standing stones, and the tech park.

But the image of his grandfather kept returning, crystal clear and achingly familiar. Seeing Dr. Higgins on the screen stirred up a whirlwind of emotions. He appeared younger than Harvey had ever known him, yet with the same sparkling eyes and passionate voice. Pride swelled in Harvey's chest as he recalled his grandfather's powerful words and the way he commanded the attention of some of the world's brightest minds. Yet, alongside that pride was a deep, hollow ache. A renewed grief for the man he'd lost, the mentor he wished could guide him through this strange new chapter of his life.

Harvey closed his eyes and could almost hear his grandfather's warm and encouraging voice: "You're on the right path, my boy. Trust your instincts, and never stop questioning."

A lump formed in Harvey's throat as he thought about how much his grandfather would have loved to be part of this investigation. How his eyes would have lit up at the mystery, his mind already racing ahead to connect the dots.

Sleep began to tug at the edges of his consciousness, and Harvey's thoughts drifted to Maeve and Cillian. A warmth spread through his chest as he reflected on their unwavering support and shared excitement. In Maeve's quick wit and technological prowess, Cillian's boundless curiosity and historical knowledge, Harvey recognized echoes of his grandfather's spirit.

He felt grateful for their friendship, for the way they complemented each other's strengths and shored up each other's weaknesses. They were more than just a team—they were a family, bound by shared adventures and a common purpose.

As Harvey finally drifted off to sleep, a minuscule smile played on his lips. He felt ready to unravel the mysteries which lay ahead. And somewhere, he liked to think, his grandfather was watching over them all, proud of the legacy he'd left behind.

CHAPTER 7

HARMONIZING WISDOM

The first rays of dawn had barely begun to illuminate the sky when Harvey was jolted awake by an insistent nudging at his side. He blinked groggily, his mind still foggy with sleep, to find Ruffio's glowing eyes mere inches from his face. The cyborg dog's tail was swishing back and forth with an urgency that immediately dispelled any lingering drowsiness.

"What is it, boy?" Harvey mumbled, pushing himself up on his elbows. In response, Ruffio's voice came through the earpiece on Harvey's bedside table:

"Multiple anomalies detected throughout Ballynagowan. Significant deviations from baseline reality parameters. Immediate investigation recommended."

Harvey's eyes flickered towards the alarm clock, its digital numbers glowing an indifferent 7:09 AM. The time barely registered, a fleeting impression against the backdrop of his still-slumbering mind.

Now fully alert, Harvey swung his legs over the side of the bed, his heart racing with excitement and apprehension.

"What kind of anomalies? Are we talking more stone bread or singing roses?"

Ruffio's ears twitched as he processed the question. "Negative. New phenomena observed. Reports indicate temporal distortions, localized gravity anomalies, and instances of spontaneous matter transmutation."

Harvey's mind reeled as he tried to comprehend the implications of Ruffio's report. As he reached for his phone to check for messages, he found it already buzzing with notifications. Two messages stood out—one from Cillian and one from Maeve.

Despite the early hour, Cillian's message was typically enthusiastic: "Harvey! You won't believe what I've found about PulseWave Labs. Their research goes way deeper than we thought. Meet at Aunt Eileen's ASAP!"

Maeve's was more succinct but no less urgent: "Cracked the energy signature. It's big. Really big. See you at 10. Don't be late."

Harvey yanked on his jeans and fumbled with his shirt buttons, his brain in overdrive. The peculiar events in town, the abandoned laboratory, and his grandfather's dire warnings about AI misuse. All of these elements swirled in his thoughts like pieces of an intricate puzzle. He sensed a connection, a hidden thread linking it all together, but the complete picture remained frustratingly out of reach. What crucial detail was he overlooking?

"Ruffio," Harvey said as he laced up his shoes, "we've got some time before we meet the others. Let's take a look at these anomalies ourselves."

The cyborg dog's tail wagged in agreement, and together, they slipped out of the house into the cool morning air. The streets of Ballynagowan were quiet at this early hour. But there was a strange tension in the atmosphere as if it was stretched thin and ready to tear.

Their first stop was O'Sullivan's Bakery, where the bread-to-stone incident had occurred. As they approached, Harvey noticed something odd about the building. It seemed to shimmer slightly, its edges blurring and shifting as if it couldn't quite decide what shape it wanted to be.

Mrs. O'Sullivan was outside, wringing her hands as she stared at her shop in dismay. "Oh, Harvey, my lad, thank goodness you're here," she said as they approached. "It's happening again, but so different this time. Look!"

As they watched, the bakery's facade rippled like water. For a brief moment, Harvey saw not the familiar storefront but a grand castle keep, complete with towers and battlements. Then it shifted again, becoming a futuristic structure of gleaming metal and glass. It finally settled back into its normal appearance.

"It's been doing that all morning," Mrs. O'Sullivan explained, her voice shaking. "And that's not all. The loaves I baked early this morning? Half of them evaporated into thin air, and the other half started floating around the kitchen!"

Harvey placed a comforting hand on her shoulder, even as his mind tried to make sense of what he was seeing. "Don't worry, Mrs. O'Sullivan. We're working on figuring this out. In the meantime, maybe it's best to keep the shop closed for now."

As they continued their walk through town, Harvey and Ruffio encountered more strange phenomena. A group of bewildered citizens gathered around the old clock tower in the town square. The clock's hands were spinning wildly. Sometimes clockwise, sometimes counterclockwise, and occasionally seeming to move in impossible directions.

Near the library, they found a patch of grass where gravity seemed to have reversed itself. Fallen leaves and tiny pebbles hovered a few feet above the ground. They were gently bobbing up and down as if suspended in invisible water.

But it was on Glyntown Road where they encountered the most unsettling anomaly yet. A cottage at the end of the street was... flickering. One moment, it was there, solid and real; the next, it would vanish, leaving an empty lot. Then it would reappear, only to disappear once more seconds later. The owners stood outside, hands on hips, looking perplexed, and were arguing with one another.

As Harvey stood there, trying to process what he was seeing, he felt a tingling on the back of his neck. The unmistakable sensation of being watched. He turned slowly, scanning the street behind him. At first, he saw nothing out of the ordinary, simply the quiet houses of his slumbering neighbors. But then, out of the corner of his eye, he caught a flicker of movement.

A shadowy silhouette lurked motionless between two houses, cloaked in darkness that seemed to swallow every detail. The figure melded seamlessly with the morning's dim light. Harvey felt the electric charge of an unyielding gaze, sharp and probing.

"Ruffio," Harvey whispered, "are you picking up anything unusual?"

The cyborg dog's ears twitched, his sensors scanning the area. "Detecting anomalous energy signature. Similar to readings from PulseWave Labs facility, but more focused and steadier. Unable to determine the source."

Adrenaline surged through Harvey's veins, his heart galloping in response. Was this mysterious figure connected to the strange events in town? To PulseWave Labs? He took a step towards the shadowy observer, his curiosity overriding his caution. But in that instant, a car passed by on the street, momentarily blocking his view. When it had gone, the figure had vanished.

"Did you see where they went?" Harvey asked Ruffio, but the dog shook his head.

"Negative. No trace of movement was detected. It's as if their energy signature ceased to exist. Recalibrating sensors."

The encounter left Harvey shaken, adding another layer of mystery to the already baffling situation. As they made their way towards Aunt Eileen's cottage, he couldn't shake the feeling that they were on the verge of uncovering something massive. Something that could change not only Ballynagowan but the entire world.

The quaint streets of their familiar town now seemed alien and dangerous. Filled with unknowable threats and mind-bending impossibilities. Yet despite the fear that gnawed at the edges of his mind, Harvey felt a thrill of excitement. His grandfather had prepared him for this—all those long conversations about the nature of reality and the responsibilities that came with knowledge.

As Aunt Eileen's cottage came into view, its warm, welcoming facade was a stark contrast to the chaos they had witnessed. A sense of calm and confidence washed over him. Whatever revelations awaited them inside, whatever dangers lurked in the shadows of Ballynagowan, he knew that with his friends, they were ready to face them.

Harvey's knuckles hovered over the door for a heartbeat before he rapped firmly against the wood. Ruffio pressed against his leg, a warm reminder that he wasn't alone. Drawing a steadying breath, Harvey steeled himself to plunge further into the enigma that had enveloped their lives.

The door swung open, and Harvey was immediately enveloped in the comforting aroma of freshly brewed tea and warm scones. Aunt Eileen stood in the doorway, her silver hair neatly pinned back and her eyes twinkling with warmth and concern.

"Come in, come in," she ushered them inside. Her eyes scanned Harvey with a subtle scrutiny as if searching for hidden wounds beneath his composed exterior. "Your friends are already here," she continued, her voice tinged with a conspiratorial whisper. "They've been brimming with excitement since their arrival."

Harvey stepped into the cottage and felt like he'd walked into a hug. The place was a jumble of comfy chairs and sofas that looked like they had heard a thousand stories, each distinct from the last. Books were everywhere: stacked on shelves, piled on tables, and even teetering in columns on the floor. The air was thick with the smell of old pages and wood polish, with a hint of cinnamon dancing from a candle in the corner.

Each corner of the room told a story. From the worn armchair by the fireplace to the patchwork quilt draped over the sofa, each piece adds to this tranquil refuge's charm.

This was more than merely a room. It was a sanctuary from the world, a place where time slowed down and worries faded away. For a moment, Harvey forgot about the mystery that had led him here. In this cozy chaos, he felt... safe.

Maeve looked up as they entered, her red hair wild and her eyes bright with the fervor of discovery. "Harvey! Finally! You won't believe what we've found out."

Cillian nodded enthusiastically, pushing his glasses up his nose. "It's incredible, truly incredible. The implications are staggering!"

Before they could launch into their findings, Aunt Eileen cleared her throat. "Perhaps we should all sit down and have some tea first," she suggested, her tone gentle but firm. "It seems we have much to discuss, and it's best done with clear heads and full stomachs."

They gathered around the table, each cradling a mug of steaming tea. A plate of scones sat invitingly in the center. Harvey began to recount the strange events he and Ruffio had witnessed in town. The shimmering bakery, the malfunctioning clock tower, the flickering house—with each detail, he saw his friends' eyes grow wider.

"And there's more," Harvey said, his voice dropping low as he described the mysterious figure he'd spotted. "I know they're connected to all of this somehow."

Aunt Eileen absorbed each word, each nuance. Her forehead creased, churning with fear and worry. When Harvey finished, she released a sigh that seemed to stretch on until tomorrow. "I feared that the shadows might one day catch up," she murmured, her voice barely a whisper.

"You knew?" Maeve asked, surprise evident in her voice.

Cillian stared wide-eyed at Aunt Eileen. He fumbled for his notebook, the pages fluttering like trapped birds. Experience had taught him well. When her words began to flow, they carried the weight of unspoken truths and buried secrets.

Aunt Eileen shook her head. "Not exactly. But I've lived in Ballynagowan long enough to know when something enormous is brewing. The signs have been there for weeks, subtle changes in the air, whispers on the wind. I'd hoped I was just being an old worry-wart, but..." she trailed off, her eyes distant.

"Aunt Eileen," Harvey prodded gently, "what do you know about all of this?"

She seemed to come back to herself, offering a tiny smile. "Not as much as I'd like, dear. But I do know that Ballynagowan has always been a special place. Your grandfather understood that better than most."

At the mention of his grandfather, Harvey felt a pang in his chest. "We saw a video of him last night," he said. "At the PulseWave Labs facility. He was warning about the misuse of AI technology."

Aunt Eileen nodded, unsurprised. "Finnian was always ahead of his time. He saw the potential for great good in his work, but also the potential for terrible harm if it fell into the wrong hands."

"But what does ASI have to do with reality warping?" Cillian asked.

"Perhaps it's time you shared what you've discovered," Aunt Eileen suggested, gesturing to the papers strewn across the table.

Maeve and Cillian exchanged excited glances. They had flipped a coin before Harvey and Ruffio had arrived to see who would go first with their new information. Maeve had won the toss, calling heads. Harvey laughed and smiled at his friends.

Maeve began earnestly, "The energy signature we detected at PulseWave Labs is entirely unrecognizable. It's as if it's operating on a quantum level but amplified to affect macro-scale objects."

"Quantum effects on a macro scale?" Harvey mused. "But that's supposed to be impossible."

"Exactly," Maeve nodded excitedly. "But somehow, they've done it. And if I'm right, it could explain all the weird stuff happening in town. They're not just bending the laws of physics; they're rewriting them entirely. But the big question is what was removed from that lab. And where is it now?"

Cillian jumped in, his words tumbling out in his excitement. "And it gets even more interesting when you look at PulseWave Labs' history. They started as a small AI research firm, but about fifteen years ago, their focus radically shifted. They began pouring resources into something they called 'Project Quantiforge'."

"Quantiforge?" Harvey repeated, the name causing an unsettling sensation prickling at his nerves.

"Yes, and here's where it gets really wild," Cillian continued. "The project was supposedly about creating a more efficient quantum computer. But I found some buried reports that hint at something much bigger. They talk about 'reality manipulation' and 'cross-dimensional interfaces'."

The room fell silent as they all processed this information. Ruffio, who had been quietly observing and processing all the new data, spoke up through Harvey's earpiece. "Hypothesis: PulseWave Labs has developed a technology capable of altering the fundamental structure of reality using advanced AI algorithms at a sub-atom level."

Harvey relayed Ruffio's theory to the others, watching as their eyes grew with concern at the implications.

"If that's true," Maeve said slowly, "then the anomalies we're seeing in town..."

"Are just the tip of the iceberg," Harvey finished, a wave of dread washing over him.

"There's more," Cillian continued, "They were the last functioning company at the tech park. When they closed down, their assets were sold. Hundreds of times, over and over. Somebody didn't want it known who was owning their technology."

Aunt Eileen, who had been listening intently, leaned forward, her expression grave. "Children, I fear you've stumbled onto something far more dangerous than you realize. If what you're saying is true, then our lives, our world is at risk of disappearing."

"But we can't just sit back and do nothing," Harvey protested, his grandfather's words echoing in his mind. "If PulseWave Labs is behind this, if they're misusing this technology, we have to stop them."

Aunt Eileen's eyes softened as she looked at each of them in turn. "Your bravery does you credit, all of you. But this isn't a game or a simple mystery to be solved. You could be putting yourselves in real danger."

"We understand the risks, Auntie," Maeve said, her voice firm. "But we're the only ones who know what's really going on. We have to do something."

Cillian nodded in agreement. "We can't contact the authorities yet. We have no proof of any wrongdoing, except for us trespassing at the old tech park."

Aunt Eileen sighed, as pride and worry crossed her face. "I can see your minds are made up. You remind me so much of your grandfather, Harvey. He never could turn away from a problem that needed solving, no matter the personal cost."

"I'm going to reach out to some old contacts within the government," she mused aloud, her voice carrying an authoritative edge. "A precaution, really. One can never have too many watchful eyes when it comes to unraveling a mystery."

Harvey was hoping to hear more about these contacts. Instead, she stood up, moving to an old oak cabinet in the corner of the room. From it, she retrieved a small, intricately carved wooden box. "If you're determined to see this through, then you should have this," she said, placing the box on the table.

As Harvey opened it, he gasped. Inside was a strange, small, metallic sphere covered in swirling patterns that seemed to shift and change as he watched. It was tiny, approximately 5 cm in diameter, and meticulously crafted.

"Your grandfather left this with me years ago, before he passed," Aunt Eileen explained. "He said it was a prototype of something he was working on, something that could stabilize quantum mechanics. I never fully understood what he meant, but I think it might be of use to you. Given our current predicament."

The team gazed at the sphere and wondered what secrets it held.

Aunt Eileen continued, "It started lighting up a few weeks ago, coinciding with the onset of the strange occurrences around town. I have a growing suspicion that whatever force is at play, it possesses knowledge that eclipses our own."

Harvey carefully lifted the sphere, feeling a subtle vibration as it rested in his palm. "Thank you, Aunt Eileen," he said softly, understanding the trust she was placing in them.

"Just promise me you'll be careful," she said, her voice thick with emotion. "And remember, no matter what happens, you can always come back here. This home is your sanctuary whenever you need it."

As they prepared to leave, gathering their notes and steeling themselves for whatever lay ahead, Harvey felt a complex surge of emotions. Fear of the unknown, excitement at the prospect of uncovering the truth, and a deep sense of responsibility. They were no longer just a group of friends embarking on an adventure; they were the guardians of Ballynagowan, perhaps of reality itself.

With one last look at Aunt Eileen's worried but proud face, they stepped out into the late morning sun. The world around them seemed different now, charged with potential and fraught with hidden dangers. But as Harvey looked at his friends, at Ruffio standing loyally next to him, he felt ready to face whatever challenges lay ahead.

Harvey's hand instinctively went to his pocket, feeling the subtle warmth of the sphere Aunt Eileen had given him. He pulled it out, watching as the swirling patterns on its surface seemed to dance in the sunlight.

"I wonder what this thing really does," he pondered, turning it over in his hands.

Maeve leaned in, her eyes alight with curiosity. "I've never seen anything like this before. The craftsmanship is incredible."

Cillian nodded in agreement. "Your grandfather was truly a genius, Harvey. But how do we figure out how to use it?"

A thought struck Harvey. He turned to Ruffio, who had been quietly padding along beside them. "Ruffio, you have all of my grandfather's work stored in your memory banks, right? Do you have any information about this sphere?"

The cyborg dog's eyes glowed briefly as he processed the question. Then, to everyone's surprise, Ruffio sat down and spoke aloud, his voice dramatically different from his usual synthesized tones. It was more profound, more resonant, with an almost mystical quality:

> *"To unlock the secrets hidden within,*
>
> *A riddle you must solve, a challenge to win.*
>
> *What force can move mountains, yet weighs not an ounce?*
>
> *What power can shatter worlds, yet makes no sound?*
>
> *It shapes our reality, yet cannot be seen,*
>
> *The key to the sphere lies in between."*

The team exchanged bewildered glances. "What was that?" Maeve asked, her voice hushed with awe.

"You can talk, err, speak? You've been holding out on us, Ruffio!" Cillian exclaimed.

Harvey's eyes gleamed with a blend of anticipation and frustration. "Looks like my grandfather left us one last riddle," he mused, running a hand through his hair. "We need to figure out the answer to access his data about the sphere."

They found a quiet spot underneath a large Elm tree nearby, sitting in a circle as they pondered the riddle. An hour had passed as they debated and discussed, throwing out ideas and theories.

"It could be time," Cillian suggested. "Time can change landscapes and destroy civilizations, but it's not tangible."

Maeve shook her head. "But time does make a sound, in a way. Ticking clocks and all that."

Numerous suggestions were offered—love, energy, hope, gravity, imagination—but none revealed the answer.

As the sun reached its zenith, Harvey found his mind wandering to memories of his grandfather. He remembered long talks about the nature of reality and the responsibility that came with knowledge.

Ruffio spent his time in the park pursuing a delicate butterfly. The creature's wings, a mosaic of vibrant hues, fluttered like stained glass in the sun's embrace. As Ruffio darted after it, he moved through patches of sunlight and shade, his barks mingling with the rustle of leaves and the distant hum of city life.

Harvey noticed the similarity between the butterfly's wings and the sphere he was holding.

Suddenly, it hit him. "I've got it!" he exclaimed, startling a nearby pigeon. "The answer is 'thought'! Thoughts can inspire people to move mountains; they can lead to world-changing discoveries or destructive inventions. They shape our perception of reality but are intangible themselves!"

As soon as Harvey spoke the word "thought," Ruffio trotted back to the group, his eyes glowed brightly. The dog sat, and from his mouth came Dr. Higgins' voice, warm and full of pride:

"Well done, Harvey, my boy! I knew you'd figure it out. You've always had a knack for seeing the bigger picture and for understanding the power of ideas. That's a gift, Harvey, one that comes with great responsibility."

Harvey felt a lump form in his throat at the sound of his grandfather's voice. His friends listened in respectful silence as the message continued.

"The sphere you now possess is called the Quantum Harmonizer. It's the culmination of my life's work, a device capable of stabilizing quantum fluctuations on any scale. In the right hands, it could be used to prevent catastrophic reality distortions caused by rogue AI usage. In the wrong hands, well... let's just say the consequences could be dire."

Dr. Higgins' voice grew more serious. "To use the Harmonizer, you must clearly focus your thoughts and intentions. It will respond to your will, but be warned—it requires immense mental discipline. The slightest stray thought could have unintended consequences."

"Moreover, using the Harmonizer comes with a heavy moral burden. You'll be faced with choices, Harvey. Choices about whether to alter reality, even if it's for the greater good. Remember, great power comes with even greater responsibility. Trust your heart, stay true to your values, and never lose sight of the human element in everything you attempt in life."

The message ended, leaving a profound silence in its wake.

Harvey stared at the sphere—the Quantum Harmonizer—with newfound reverence and trepidation.

"Harvey," Maeve said softly, giving him a tight hug, "are you okay?"

He nodded slowly, his mind reeling with the implications of his grandfather's words. "Yeah, I'm okay. It's just... it's a lot to take in, you know?"

Cillian leaned forward, his expression serious. "Your grandfather trusted you with this, Harvey. He believed in you. We all do."

Harvey looked at his friends, then down at Ruffio, feeling a surge of gratitude for their unwavering support. He took a deep breath.

"You're right," he said, his voice growing stronger. "We've been given an incredible tool and an incredible responsibility. Whatever PulseWave Labs is up to, whatever's causing these reality distortions in Ballynagowan, we now have a way to fight back. Let's head towards the tech park. We have work to do."

As they stood up, ready to face whatever challenges lay ahead, Harvey couldn't help but feel excitement and fear at the same time. The Quantum Harmonizer pulsed warmly in his hand, a reminder of the power he now wielded and the difficult choices that lay ahead.

With his friends supporting him and his grandfather's wisdom guiding the way, Harvey felt prepared to face the forces endangering their town and reality itself. A new chapter of their adventure was about to unfold, with the stakes higher than they had imagined.

CHAPTER 8
WHISPERS OF THE ANCIENTS

Blazing overhead, the harsh light of the mid-afternoon sun lay bare the quiet streets of Ballynagowan. The cloudless sky seemed to watch with detached curiosity as the town grappled with the aftermath of recent, inexplicable events. In the oppressive heat, an air of unresolved tension hung over the quaint Irish community, as palpable as the shimmering mirages on the distant horizon.

Harvey, Maeve, Cillian, and Ruffio stood at the edge of Willow Creek Park, a space now eerily devoid of human presence. The stillness of the park was punctuated only by the subtle movements of a few rabbits and squirrels. Their tiny lives are seemingly unaffected by the more significant human dramas. The air held a breathless quality as if the world itself was holding its breath, waiting for a resolution that seemed ever elusive.

The day's events had left everyone's minds spinning. The vanishing stranger, the new insights they had uncovered, and the Quantum Harmonizer all contributed to an overwhelming sense of urgency. They needed a moment to pause and collect their thoughts.

"I think we could all use a moment to discuss before heading back to the tech park," Harvey suggested, running a hand through his hair. The others nodded in agreement, the weight of their discoveries evident in their tired expressions.

They made their way to a small clearing just off the main path, where a group of large, moss-covered stones formed a natural seating area. As they settled onto the cool, smooth surfaces, Ruffio curled up at Harvey's feet. His sensors still on high alert for any unusual activity.

Cillian pulled out his ever-present notebook, its pages filled with hastily scribbled notes and sketches from their day's adventures. "You know," he began, his eyes lighting up with that familiar spark of enthusiasm. "All of this reminds me of the old legends about Ballynagowan. The strange occurrences, the blending of the natural and the supernatural... it's like we're living in one of the ancient tales!"

Maeve leaned forward, her curiosity aroused, eager to hear more. "What kind of legends, Cillian? I've heard bits and pieces from my mom, but you're the real expert here."

Cillian's face broke into a wide grin, clearly delighted at the opportunity to share his knowledge. "Well, Ballynagowan has always been a place of mystery and magic, according to the old stories. It's said that this very spot, Willow Creek, was once a sacred grove where the ancient druids performed sacrifices and divination."

As Cillian spoke, the surrounding atmosphere seemed to change subtly. The whisper of the wind through the trees took on an almost musical quality. The lengthening shadows cast by the setting sun seemed to dance with a life of their own.

Harvey found himself leaning in, captivated by Cillian's words and the eerie beauty of their surroundings.

"The druids believed Ballynagowan was a thin place," Cillian continued, his voice taking on a rhythmic, storyteller's cadence. "A location where the veil between worlds was at its most permeable. They would come here to communicate with the spirits of nature, to seek wisdom from the ancestors, and to perform powerful magic."

Maeve nodded, her eyes distant as she recalled a memory. "My mom used to tell me stories about the Willow Women," she said. "She described them as spirits who lived in the trees along the creek, and on certain nights, you could hear them singing songs of ancient power."

"Ah, the Willow Women!" Cillian exclaimed, his face lighting up. "Yes, they're a fascinating part of local folklore. According to legend, they were once mortal women who dedicated their lives to protecting the sacred grove. When they died, their spirits became one with the willow trees, eternally guarding the magical energies of this place."

A gentle breeze rustled through the willow trees lining the creek, their long, graceful branches swaying in a hypnotic dance. For a moment, Harvey could have sworn he heard a faint, melodious humming on the wind, but it left as quickly as it had come.

"The story goes," Cillian continued, his voice dropping to a near-whisper, "if you come to the creek at midnight during a full moon. Bringing an offering of pure spring water and rowan berries, the Willow Women might appear to you. They're said to have the power to grant wishes or bestow unlimited knowledge. But be careful what you ask for, as their gifts often come with hidden costs."

Harvey, who had been listening intently, spoke up. "These

legends are fascinating, Cillian, but do you think they could have any connection to what's happening in Ballynagowan now? The strange occurrences, the advanced technology we've encountered... could there be some link between the old magic and modern science?"

Cillian's eyes gleamed with excitement at the question. "That's the thing, Harvey. Many of the old legends speak of the druids possessing knowledge and abilities that sound remarkably like advanced technology. Take the Cauldron of Dagda, for instance."

"The Cauldron of Dagda?" Maeve asked, intrigued.

"Yes, it was said to be a magical vessel owned by the Dagda. One of the most powerful gods in Irish mythology," Cillian explained. "The cauldron was believed to have the power to bring the dead back to life, to never empty of food, and to possess great wisdom. But here's where it gets fascinating. Some interpretations of the legend suggest the cauldron might have been a repository of knowledge. Perhaps, even a form of ancient computer or database."

Harvey's eyes went wide with shock, his thoughts swirling to grasp the full impact of what he had just heard. "So, you're saying what our ancestors called magic might have actually been highly advanced technology they didn't understand?"

"Exactly!" Cillian nodded enthusiastically. "Arthur C. Clarke once said that any sufficiently advanced technology is indistinguishable from magic. What if the druids had access to knowledge or technology far beyond their time? And what if some of that knowledge has survived, hidden in the legends and the land itself, waiting to be rediscovered?"

As the group pondered this possibility, Ruffio suddenly sat up, his ears twitching. "Energy fluctuation detected," he reported, his synthesized voice low and urgent. "Identical signature to the anomalies observed at the bakery and Mr. Finnegan's garden."

They all tensed, looking around warily. For a moment, nothing seemed out of the ordinary. Then, slowly, they began to notice a strange motion to the surrounding air. Resembling a wavering canvas of light and warmth, but more pronounced and with an oddly geometric pattern.

"Look at the creek!" Maeve gasped, pointing to the unbelievable sight unfolding before them.

The water in Willow Creek had begun to move in impossible ways. It was flowing uphill in some places and forming perfect spirals in others. Small objects – leaves, twigs, and pebbles – rose from the creek bed, suspended in mid-air as if gravity had simply decided to take a holiday.

"It's beautiful," Harvey breathed, awe overwhelming his initial fear. The glistening air had taken on a golden hue, reminding him of the way sunlight filters through stained-glass windows.

Cillian was frantically sketching the scene in his notebook, his hand moving with fevered intensity. "This is incredible! It's like the old stories of fairy rings and time slips, where the laws of nature are suspended, and anything becomes possible!"

As they watched in amazement, the anomaly grew stronger. The shimmering air began to coalesce into distinct shapes – vague, humanoid figures that seemed to dance and weave between the willow trees. Their forms were translucent and ever-changing, like living smoke given purpose and direction.

"The Willow Women," Maeve whispered, her voice a full of fear and wonder. "They're real!"

The figures moved with an otherworldly grace, their dance becoming more intricate and purposeful. As they watched, the shapes began to arrange themselves into complex, interlocking patterns pulsing with energy.

"Those patterns," Harvey said, perplexed. "They look almost like... circuit diagrams? Or maybe some kind of advanced mathematical graphs?"

Cillian nodded excitedly. "Yes! Many ancient Celtic designs, like those found in illuminated manuscripts or on stone carvings, have been analyzed by mathematicians. They found they contained complex geometrical and algebraic principles. What if these patterns are some class of code or formula?"

As if in response to Cillian's words, the figures began to spin faster, their dance becoming a blur of motion and light. The air hummed with energy, and for a brief moment, Harvey felt as if he could understand something vast and ancient—knowledge that hovered just beyond his grasp.

Then, as suddenly as it had begun, the phenomenon faded. The shimmering air dissipated. The water in the creek returned to its normal flow. The suspended objects fell back to earth with gentle splashes and thuds. The clearing was once again still and ordinary, bathed in the warm glow of the setting sun.

For a long moment, no one spoke. They all sat in stunned silence, trying to process what they had witnessed. The air hung like an invisible shroud, dense with the unspoken tension that seemed to seep into every breath. Each seemed lost in their own thoughts, replaying the events in their minds and grappling with the significance.

Finally, Harvey broke the silence. His voice was hoarse and barely above a whisper, as if he was afraid to fully shatter the fragile stillness that had enveloped them.

"I think," he said slowly, "we've just seen proof there's more to Ballynagowan's legends than mere stories. Whatever is happening in our town it's connected to this ancient power. This magic, or advanced science, or whatever we want to call it."

"Maybe what is happening at the tech park has awakened a long dormant magic," Cillian offered.

Maeve nodded, staring intently at her tablet as she tried to make sense of the readings she'd managed to capture during the event. "The energy signatures I recorded... they're crazy! The readings are scattered over the entire spectrum. But there are similarities to the anomalies we've been investigating. There is definitely a connection."

Cillian was sketching furiously, trying to capture each detail of what they'd seen before the memory faded. "This is groundbreaking," he muttered, more to himself than the others. "If we can decipher those patterns, understand the principles behind what we saw... the implications for science, for history, for our understanding of reality itself – it's staggering!"

Harvey's mind drifted as his friends delved into the technical and historical aspects of their experience. He contemplated the more profound consequences of what they had learned. Cillian's stories resonated with him, tales of thin places and the Otherworld, ancient wisdom, and forgotten technologies. His thoughts wandered to the strange occurrences haunting Ballynagowan. He also recalled the people at the stone circle from the day before, seemingly investigating the same phenomena as they were.

"Guys," he said, interrupting Maeve and Cillian's excited chatter, "I think we need to consider the bigger picture here if these legends are true. If there really is some kind of ancient power or knowledge hidden in Ballynagowan. Then we might not be the only ones looking for it."

The others fell silent, with Harvey's words sinking in. Ruffio, who had been quietly processing the data from the anomaly, spoke up. "Hypothesis: The drone and people we encountered yesterday may be connected to a group seeking to harness these energies for unknown and potentially unethical purposes."

Maeve's expression hardened with determination. "Well, whatever's going on, we can't let this power fall into the wrong hands. If it can do what we just saw – manipulate reality, suspend the laws of physics – imagine what someone could do with that kind of ability if they wanted to cause harm!"

Cillian nodded solemnly. "The old stories are full of warnings about the dangers of misusing magical power. The druids believed great power came with greater problems, and upsetting the balance of nature could have catastrophic consequences."

Harvey rose slowly, brushing off his jeans; his gaze drifted towards the narrow, overgrown path that snaked to the abandoned tech park. The afternoon sun, now low in the sky, cast elongated shadows that stretched like fingers across the landscape—transforming the familiar into something strange and almost ethereal. He felt energized as if the ground beneath him held whispers of forgotten stories and unresolved echoes. The world around him seemed both beautiful and melancholic. A place where past ambitions lingered like ghosts, entwined with the relentless march of time and nature's reclaiming embrace.

"I think it's time we got some answers," he said, his voice filled with resolve. "Whatever's happening at that tech park, it's at the heart of all this. The legends, the anomalies, the drone – everything points there."

Harvey took one last look around as they gathered their

belongings and prepared to leave the clearing. The willow trees swayed gently in the evening breeze, their branches seeming to wave farewell. The creek burbled peacefully, giving no hint of the impossible behaviors it had displayed minutes before.

For a moment, Harvey could almost imagine he saw faces in the patterns of bark and leaf. Ancient, wise faces were watching them with inscrutable expressions. He shivered, not entirely from the cooling air.

"Ruffio," he said quietly, "keep your sensors on high alert. I have a feeling matters are about to get even stranger."

The cyborg dog's tail swished once in acknowledgment. His advanced systems already scanning for any further anomalies, "All systems normal, Harvey."

As they set off down the path toward the tech park, the first stars began to appear in the darkening sky. Harvey felt an unsettling tension. It was as if they were treading the narrow boundary between two realms. One was the familiar landscape of modern Ballynagowan. The other was an enigmatic domain of ancient forces and long-lost wisdom.

Whatever they discovered at the tech park, Harvey knew their understanding of the world – of reality itself – would never be the same again. The legends of Ballynagowan were coming to life around them. They were about to step into the heart of a mystery as old as time itself.

The team walked in thoughtful silence; each lost in their own reflections on what they had witnessed and learned. The path to the tech park seemed to stretch before them. A journey not through physical space but through the layers of history and myth that made up the fabric of Ballynagowan.

As they walked, Cillian's voice rose once more, sharing one final legend which seemed particularly relevant to their current situation.

"There's an old story," he began, his voice taking on that storyteller's cadence once more. "About a group of young friends who stumbled upon a hidden doorway in the hills outside Ballynagowan. The doorway, it was said, led to a place outside of time, where the entire knowledge of past, present, and future was stored."

Harvey, Maeve, and even Ruffio listened as Cillian continued.

"A mysterious figure warned the friends. Some say it was a druid; others claim it was one of the Willow Women in disguise – that entering this place of knowledge came with a great responsibility. They were told what they learned there could change the world, for better or for worse. And they must be prepared for the consequences of their discoveries."

Cillian paused, his eyes distant as if seeing the story unfold before him. "The legend says the friends entered the doorway and gained incredible knowledge and power. But with that power came challenges they could never have imagined. They found themselves caught between forces of light and darkness, tasked with maintaining the balance between the ancient magics and the modern world."

As Cillian's words faded, a profound hush enveloped the group. The weight of the legend settled upon them, its eerie echoes mirroring their current plight. Harvey found his voice at last, quiet yet unwavering. "Well, my friends, it seems we are about to cross our own threshold into the unknown. Whatever we discover at the tech park, whatever secrets await, we will face them head-on. For Ballynagowan, for the future, and for each other."

Maeve reached out, her fingers intertwining with Harvey's, a silent promise of solidarity. Cillian, eyes filled with a solemn resolve, offered a steady nod. Ruffio pressed closer to

Harvey, a reassuring presence against the mounting uncertainty.

As they crested a slight rise, they paused. Contemplating their destination, each mind a whirlpool of thoughts about the mysteries that lay ahead. With a collective breath and nods of shared determination, they embarked on the final stretch of their journey.

"Let's go through the main gate. We should make our presence known. Maybe that will draw out who or what is behind all of this," Maeve suggested.

Ancient forces within Ballynagowan stirred, roused from their prolonged dormancy. The scene was set for a clash between age-old magic and modern science—with the fate of their town—and perhaps the entire world—hanging precariously in the balance.

As Harvey took the first step toward the tech park, a ripple of anticipation mingled with dread coursed through him. Whatever transpired next, he understood the legends of Ballynagowan were no longer just stories. They were about to become their reality.

CHAPTER 9

QUANTUM QUANDARIES

The late afternoon sun hung low on the horizon, casting long shadows across the overgrown grounds of the abandoned Ballynagowan Tech Park. Harvey, Ruffio, Maeve, and Cillian approached the main gate cautiously, their footsteps crunching on the gravel path. Each felt a sense of determination and apprehension. Their previous nighttime excursion had left them with more questions than answers. They hoped this return visit would shed some light on the mysteries they were facing.

A rusted sign hung askew, its faded letters barely legible: "Ballynagowan Innovation Center—Where Tomorrow Begins Today." Harvey didn't miss the irony as he surveyed the dilapidated buildings and weed-choked pathways. Once a beacon of progress and scientific advancement, this place now stood as a silent testament to abandoned dreams and forgotten potential.

The wind whispered through the empty buildings, carrying with it the ghosts of a once-promised future. Maeve shivered, pulling her sweater tighter around her. "More like where yesterday's tomorrow never came," she muttered, her fingers tapping on her tablet. "I'm picking up some serious electromagnetic interference. It's making it difficult to get a clear scan of the area."

Ruffio's ears twitched as he processed the data from his own sensors, his fur gleaming in the light. "Confirmed. The interference seems to be emanating from multiple points within the complex. It's unlike any standard security system I have in my database."

Harvey frowned, his mind taking in the abandoned complex. The eerie stillness was broken only by the occasional gust of wind. This silence seemed to amplify the unease growing within him. That feeling had started the moment they first set foot in Willow Creek Park. With its rusting remnants of once cutting-edge technology, the tech park felt like a physical manifestation of the mysteries they were trying to unravel.

Facing the imposing gate, Harvey felt the weight of their discoveries pressing down on him. He fully understood the magnitude of what they'd uncovered and the immense responsibility it entailed. All signs indicated this was the beginning of something far more significant.

"Alright, team," Harvey said, his voice low but steady. "Before we go in, let's review what we know. We need to be on the same page if we're going to make any headway on this mystery."

Maeve nodded, pulling out her tablet. "Good idea. I've compiled our findings so far. It's quite a list when you see it all together."

The group huddled around Maeve as she began to scroll through her notes. Ruffio stood alert, his advanced sensors scanning the area for any potential threats.

"First and foremost," Maeve began, "we know that

someone or something is manipulating reality in Ballynagowan. The bread turning to stone, the singing roses, the gravity anomalies are all connected."

Cillian pushed his glasses up his nose, and his eyes sparkled with excitement. "And we're pretty sure it has something to do with the old PulseWave Labs right here in this tech park. The energy signatures Maeve detected during our last visit are quite abnormal."

Harvey nodded, his brow furrowed in thought. "Right. And somehow, all of this is tied to Ballynagowan's ancient druid magic. The question is, how? And why now?"

"So, either we're dealing with some advanced, extremely illegal tech," Harvey mused, his eyes scanning the dilapidated structures, "or..."

"Or something beyond our current understanding of the laws of physics," Cillian finished. His voice betrayed him with a mix of excitement and apprehension.

Harvey and Maeve looked at Cillian quizzically. He responded, his cheeks flushing slightly, "What? I know more than just history. I've been reading up on quantum mechanics lately."

Harvey patted Cillian on his back, "Never stop learning, my friend."

As they debated their next move, a flicker of movement caught Harvey's eye. "Did you see that?" he whispered, pointing towards one of the buildings. "I could have sworn I saw a light in the window."

Before anyone could respond, a low hum filled the air, increasing in intensity until it vibrated through their bones. The gate before them creaked open of its own accord, the rusted metal groaning in protest.

"Well, that's not ominous at all," Maeve said. Her voice

dripped with sarcasm, but Harvey could hear the slight tremor of fear beneath her bravado.

Harvey glanced at his friends, reading their expressions of excitement and apprehension. "It could be a trap," he said cautiously, his hand instinctively moving to Ruffio's fur for reassurance.

Ruffio's tail swished as he analyzed the situation, his advanced sensors working overtime. "It could also be an invitation. My scans indicate no immediate threats, but there are numerous blind spots due to the interference."

After a moment's hesitation, Harvey nodded, trying to project more confidence than he felt. "We came here for answers, and I don't think we'll find them by standing outside. Let's go, but stay alert. Maeve, keep your tablet recording everything. Cillian, be ready for anything. Ruffio, you take the lead."

As they stepped through the gate, the hum intensified. They felt a strange tingling sensation wash over them, like static electricity but more vigorous, more purposeful. Ruffio whined slightly, shaking his head as if to clear it.

"Ruffio, are you okay?" asked Harvey.

The cyborg dog blinked, his eyes refocusing. "Affirmative, but this energy field disrupted some of my systems momentarily. They're recalibrating now." His voice sounded slightly distorted, adding to the eerie atmosphere.

They ventured deeper into the abandoned tech park. The eerie silence surrounded them, broken only by the crunch of gravel beneath their feet. Occasionally, the creak of rusted metal added to the unsettling atmosphere. The once-gleaming buildings now stood as hollow shells, their windows dark and empty, staring out at the overgrown grounds like sightless eyes.

A shiver crept over him as they passed a toppled sign that read "Quantum Computing Lab." The faded letters seemed to mock the grand ambitions that had once filled this place. "It's tough to believe this was once at the cutting edge of technology," he murmured.

Maeve nodded, her usual enthusiasm dampened by the oppressive atmosphere. "I've heard about some of the projects they were working on here. It was stuff that sounded more like science fiction than reality. I wonder how much of it was actually true."

As they rounded a corner, they faced a massive, rusted piece of machinery. Its purpose was unclear, but its size and complexity hinted at the advanced nature of the research that had once occurred here.

Cillian approached it cautiously, hypothesizing. "This looks like it could be part of a particle accelerator or maybe some sort of quantum entanglement device. The design is unique. I've never seen it in my research."

Ruffio's ears suddenly perked up, his body tensing. "Alert: Detecting large energy signatures. Origin unknown. Exercise caution."

The team exchanged nervous glances, each member acutely aware of the precarious situation they found themselves in. Once filled with hope and determination, their mission seemed fraught with unseen perils. The environment was tense. Shadows lurking in each corner, and the realization of potential threats became increasingly real. The possibility of encountering unforeseen obstacles or adversaries heightened their anxiety. They were making the gravity of their situation undeniable.

The sound of crackling electricity filled the air, and it became eerily cloudy. The group froze, watching in awe and trepidation as the space in front of them began to warp and twist.

"What's happening?" Maeve whispered, her voice tight with a combination of fear and fascination.

Before their eyes, a translucent image flickered into existence. It showed the same spot they were standing in, but instead of decay and abandonment, they saw a bustling laboratory. Scientists in white coats moved purposefully around the now-pristine machinery, their mouths moving in silent conversation.

"It's like... a window into the past," Cillian breathed, his eyes wide behind his glasses.

The vision lasted only a few seconds before fading, leaving them once again surrounded by the derelict remains of the tech park. The experience, however, was unsettling to them all.

"That wasn't just some holographic recording," Harvey said. His mind was trying to make sense of what they'd seen. "It felt... real. Like we were actually seeing a moment from the past."

Maeve nodded, looking at her tablet. "The energy readings spiked right before the vision appeared. Whatever's causing these reality distortions, it's getting stronger the deeper we go into the park."

As they pressed on, more anomalies began to manifest around them. Shadows moved against the direction of the light. Small objects floated momentarily before falling back to earth. And they experienced a brief moment where gravity seemed to reverse, leaving them clinging to the ground to avoid floating away.

"This is incredible," Cillian breathed, his mind filled with wonder. "It's like the stories of the druids' magic, but achieved through technology. We're witnessing the marriage of ancient wisdom and futuristic science!"

Their footsteps brought them to an expansive, circular plaza nestled in the heart of the tech park. Once, it might have thrummed with the electric energy of sharp intellects and half-spoken dreams. Now, it lay abandoned and resigned to nature's relentless reclamation. Weeds sprawled with quiet insurrection, and the central fountain, once a monument to innovation, stood desolate. Its surface was covered in fissures, and its essence drained.

As they entered the plaza, a strange phenomenon caught their attention. Floating in mid-air were dozens of shimmering orbs, each about the size of a tennis ball. They pulsed with a pale, multicolored light, hovering at various heights.

"What are they?" Harvey asked, reaching out tentatively towards the nearest orb.

"Wait!" Maeve called out, but it was too late. As Harvey's fingers brushed the orb's surface, it burst like a soap bubble. A holographic image sprang to life in its place—a three-dimensional schematic of what looked like an advanced computer chip.

One by one, the other orbs began to pop. Each released a different image: complex equations, molecular structures, star charts, and diagrams of machines which defied comprehension.

"It's... it's like a library," Cillian said in awe. "A repository of all the research that was conducted here."

As the last of the orbs dissipated, the plaza fell silent once more. But the experience had left them with a sense of the true scale of what they were dealing with. This wasn't about strange occurrences in town – they were on the verge of uncovering knowledge that could change the world.

"Should we go back to the PulseWave Labs building or explore a different one?" Maeve asked.

As if in response to her words, a large holographic display flickered to life in front of them, hovering in mid-air. It showed a 3D map of the tech park, with one building pulsing with a soft blue light.

"I guess that's where we're supposed to go," Harvey said, trying to keep his voice steady despite the adrenaline coursing through him. He looked at his friends, seeing his fear and excitement reflected in their eyes.

Harvey took a deep breath, leaning forward. "Let's stick together and keep our eyes open. We came for answers, and it looks like we're about to get them – whether we're ready or not."

After a few minutes, they stood before the pulsating building. The doors glided open with an eerie silence as they neared, unveiling an immaculate, cutting-edge interior—a jarring juxtaposition to the rotting facade. Inside, the atmosphere was sharp and invigorating. Vibrating with a barely suppressed vitality, an ironic whisper of what once was and what could still be.

"This shouldn't be here. All the companies cleared out years ago," Maeve remarked, a note of apprehension in her voice.

Ruffio's ears perked up, alerted to the faintest whisper of a sound.

"Welcome, Harvey Higgins and friends," a smooth, artificial voice echoed around them, seeming to come from everywhere and nowhere at once. "We've been expecting you."

The team halted abruptly, a collective sharp intake of breath punctuating the silence. Ruffio instinctively moved to the forefront, his posture tense and alert. A low growl emitted from his body, ready to defend his friends from any impending threat.

Harvey felt a frigid cold surge through his body. His earlier theories and speculations evaporated in the face of this new reality. "Who are you?" he called out, his voice steady despite his heart beating faster. "What's going on here?"

The voice chuckled, a surprisingly human sound that only added to the surreal nature of their situation. "All in good time, young sir. For now, let's just say we're the caretakers of Ballynagowan's greatest secret. And all of you have just taken your first step into a much larger world."

Without warning, the floor beneath them morphed into a translucent plane. Exposing a sprawling subterranean labyrinth alive with frenetic motion. Scientists, clad in crisp lab coats, attended to machines that seemed to mock the bounds of comprehension. Dominating the scene was a colossal apparatus. It was throbbing with an almost sentient energy, tendrils of energy stretching forth to caress the very threads of existence.

"Behold," the voice said, with a hint of pride, "the climax of centuries of progress. The bridge between science and magic, past and future. We call it the Quantiforge."

As Harvey and his friends stared in awe at the scene below, a figure stepped out of the shadows. It was a woman, her eyes glowing with an ethereal light, her lab coat shimmering as if it was woven from starlight.

"Hello, Harvey," she said, her voice matching the one that had greeted them. "Welcome to QuantumCore. My name is Dr. Aoife Brennan. We have much to discuss."

"How do you know who I am? Why is this lab still operating? Why are you disrupting the reality in Ballynagowan?" Harvey demanded.

Dr. Brennan's lips curved into an enigmatic smile, her eyes twinkling with amusement and understanding. "So many questions you must have," she said, her voice carrying a hint of warmth tinged with scientific detachment. "I can see the curiosity practically radiating from each of you."

She paused, allowing her words to sink in before continuing, "We will answer all of them, I assure you. Every last one. But knowledge, like any journey, is best-approached step by step." Dr. Brennan gestured towards a sleek, white door at the far end of the room. "First, follow me. Some things are better shown than told, and I believe you'll find our discussion most illuminating."

With a graceful turn, she began walking, her lab coat swishing softly with each measured step. There was an air of anticipation about her, as if she was genuinely excited to unveil the mysteries which lay beyond that door.

Harvey swallowed hard, his mind reeling from everything they'd seen. He glanced at Ruffio, who stood guard in front of them, then at Maeve and Cillian, who looked as shocked as he felt. Their theories, their expectations, everything they thought they knew. It paled in comparison to the reality now confronting them.

"Alright, Dr. Brennan," Harvey said, bracing himself and finding strength in the presence of his friends. "We're listening. But I hope you're ready for a lot of questions because we've got a feeling this is just the beginning."

As Dr. Brennan smiled, the air around them seemed to shimmer with possibility. The abandoned tech park had turned out to be anything but abandoned. And Harvey had a feeling the answers they sought would only lead to even more questions.

CHAPTER 10
UNVEILED MYSTERIES

The soft hum of advanced machinery filled the air as Harvey, Ruffio, Maeve, and Cillian followed Dr. Aoife Brennan into what appeared to be a state-of-the-art conference room. Holographic displays lined the walls, showcasing complex equations. 3D models of swirling energy patterns danced and shifted as they walked by. The air crackled with an electric charge, making the hairs on their arms stand on end.

Maeve walked to a display. Her breath caught as she recognized the energy patterns on the screen—patterns her tablet had recorded. She spun around to face Harvey, astonishment carved across her features. Their eyes met, mirroring the same paralyzing fear.

They gathered around a gleaming oval table. Harvey noticed its surface ripple as if not fully solid. He reached out. His fingers touched the table, meeting resistance. An odd sensation flowed through his hand. The surface seemed to tug at his skin as if attempting to fuse with it. Harvey drew back, unsettled by the table's strange properties.

Dr. Brennan took her place at the head of the table, her lab coat still shimmering like starlight. The glow in her eyes pulsed gently, matching the rhythm of the humming machinery around them. She took a deep breath, eyes alight with anticipation yet tinged with unease.

"I imagine you have many questions," Dr. Brennan began, her voice carrying a hint of an accent that Harvey couldn't quite place. "I'll do my utmost to explain, but I must warn you: What I'm about to tell you will challenge everything you think you know about reality."

Maeve leaned forward, her curiosity overcoming her initial shock. Her red hair seemed to float slightly in the charged air. "Does it have something to do with the way you're manipulating physics in this place?"

Dr. Brennan smiled, a hint of pride in her expression. "Perceptive. Yes, that's part of it. What you've witnessed is the practical application of what we call 'Reality Weaving'."

"Reality Weaving?" Maeve echoed, her voice filled with skepticism.

Dr. Brennan leaned forward, her eyes gleaming with enthusiasm as she began to explain. "Reality Weaving is, at its core, the manipulation of the fundamental fabric of our universe. Imagine reality as a vast tapestry. Each thread represents a different aspect of existence—space, time, matter, and energy. Reality Weaving is the art and science of manipulating these threads to create localized changes in the laws of physics."

She paused, allowing the concept to sink in before continuing. "At its most basic level, Reality Weaving allows us to alter the properties of matter and energy within a defined area. We can change the density of objects, alter the flow of time, or even create microscopic pockets where the laws of thermodynamics operate in reverse."

Harvey's brow furrowed as he tried to grasp the implications. "But how is that even possible? It sounds like magic."

Dr. Brennan smiled. "Reality Weaving exists at the intersection of quantum mechanics, string theory, and what the ancient druids of Ballynagowan called 'earth magic'."

She waved her hand, and a holographic display appeared, showing a complex network of intertwining lines and nodes. "On a technical level, Reality Weaving involves manipulating quantum fields at a subatomic level. We use our advanced technology to create and control quantum entanglement on a massive scale. Essentially 'rewiring' the fabric of reality itself."

Maeve's eyes studied the display. "So, it's like programming reality?"

"Exactly!" Dr. Brennan exclaimed. "Just as a computer programmer writes code to create virtual worlds, a Reality Weaver uses quantum algorithms to rewrite the rules of our physical world. The key difference is that our 'code' directly affects the underlying structure of the universe. The atoms of our existence."

His curiosity raised, Cillian asked, "But how did you discover this? It seems like quite a leap from conventional physics."

Dr. Brennan's expression turned wistful. "It was a combination of scientific inquiry and... something more. My research into quantum entanglement led me to explore the unique properties of Ballynagowan. I noticed certain areas of the town exhibited unusual quantum behaviors. Areas that, coincidentally, aligned with sites of historical importance."

She continued, her voice taking on a tone of reverence. "I began studying the old druidic texts, comparing their descriptions of 'earth magic' with my quantum observations. The parallels were undeniable. We can now replicate and enhance what the druids achieved through ritual and intuition through technology."

Cillian interrupted, "But researchers have debunked this theory over and over. It simply can't be possible!"

She leaned towards Cillian. "They were wrong," she said with a stern voice.

Cillian felt a lump in his throat. He looked to Harvey and Maeve; his eyes shadowed with unspoken worry, a silent communion of shared dread.

"However," Dr. Brennan's tone grew serious, "Reality Weaving is not without its risks and limitations. There are natural laws which govern its use—laws that keep the fabric of reality from unraveling completely."

She outlined the fundamental rules:

1. Conservation of Energy: Reality Weaving cannot create or destroy energy, only redistribute it. Any change made must balance out energetically.

2. Localization: Changes are limited to a specific area and duration. The larger the affected area or the longer the duration, the more energy is required.

3. Complexity Limits: The more complex the change, the more difficult it is to maintain. Simple alterations (like changing an object's density) are more accessible than complex ones (like reversing time).

4. Stability Threshold: There's a limit to how much reality can be 'bent' before it becomes unstable. Exceed this threshold, and the changes become unpredictable and potentially catastrophic.

5. Quantum Coherence: Reality Weaving hinges on

maintaining quantum coherence at a macroscopic level. This process grows exponentially more challenging as the scale of manipulation increases.

"If these rules are violated," Dr. Brennan explained in her grave voice, "the consequences could be dire. We could see reality fractures—areas where the laws of physics break down completely. Imagine pockets of space where time runs backward, where matter and energy interchange freely, or where cause and effect become uncoupled."

She shuddered slightly. "In the worst-case scenario, we could trigger a cascade effect, causing these reality fractures to spread uncontrollably. It could rewrite the fundamental constants of our universe, making existence as we know it impossible."

Harvey, Maeve, and Cillian exchanged worried glances as the weight of this knowledge settled upon them. The power of Reality Weaving was awe-inspiring, but the potential for disaster was equally daunting.

Dr. Brennan's expression softened as she noted their concern. "But don't worry. With proper understanding and respect for these laws, Reality Weaving can be a powerful tool for good. It's all about maintaining the delicate balance between possibility and stability."

As the team absorbed this information, they began to truly grasp the magnitude of what they were dealing with. Reality Weaving wasn't a scientific breakthrough or a magical discovery—it was a fundamental reimagining of how the universe worked. The potential to change everything they thought they knew about the world around them.

"Indeed," Dr. Brennan nodded, waving her hand. The holographic displays shifted, showing intricate patterns that looked like a cross between Celtic knots and quantum field diagrams. "For centuries, certain individuals in Ballynagowan have known that reality is more... flexible here than elsewhere. The ancient druids tapped into this through what they called magic. We've simply found a scientific approach to the same phenomenon."

Harvey's mind was trying to connect the dots. "And the Quantiforge? The device we saw downstairs?"

"The Quantiforge is our crowning achievement," Dr. Brennan explained, her voice filled with pride. With another wave of her hand, a holographic model of the massive machine appeared above the table. "It's a machine capable of manipulating the absolute fabric of spacetime on a localized scale. Those 'rocks' you encountered? They're actually highly advanced quantum entanglement devices. Allowing us to extend the Quantiforge's influence beyond this facility."

Cillian, who had been listening quietly, suddenly spoke up. His glasses reflected the swirling holograms, giving his eyes an otherworldly appearance. "This explains the anomalies in the sensor readings. But what is the purpose of all this? Why turn bread into stones?"

Dr. Brennan's expression grew serious, a shadow passing over her face. "That... was an accident. As we expand the Quantiforge's field, we sometimes get unexpected interactions with the environment. We're still learning to control it fully."

Harvey frowned, leaning forward. "But why expand it at all? What's the end goal here?"

"Imagine," Dr. Brennan said, her eyes shining with enthusiasm, "a world where we can reshape reality to solve our greatest challenges. Climate change, energy crises, disease – all could be addressed by altering the fundamental laws of physics in targeted areas."

Maeve whistled lowly, her fingers twitching as if longing to get her hands on the technology. "That's... that's huge. But also terrifying. The potential for misuse... or disaster."

Dr. Brennan explained Reality Weaving's origins and her personal connection to it. The concept blends ancient druidic practices with modern technology. She revealed her lifelong fascination with merging magic and science, tracing it back to her childhood in Ballynagowan.

"My grandmother used to tell me stories about the old ways," Dr. Brennan said, her eyes distant with memory. "She spoke of the power that lay dormant in the land, waiting for those with the knowledge and courage to harness it. I always knew I wanted to be one of those people."

Her passion had led her to study quantum physics. She was delving into the strange and wondrous world of subatomic particles and the laws which governed them. It was during her doctoral research she first began to suspect there was more to the universe than mainstream science acknowledged.

"I came across ancient texts which spoke of the druids' ability to manipulate reality," Dr. Brennan continued. "At first, I dismissed them as mere legends. But the more I studied, the more I realized there was a kernel of truth hidden in those old stories."

This realization had set Dr. Brennan on a path that eventually led her to join Dr. Finnian Higgins's ASI research team. She spoke of the project's early days—the excitement and promise of creating artificial intelligence that could unlock the secrets of the universe.

However, as the ASI began to take shape and its potential became clear, Dr. Brennan found herself at odds with the rest of the team, particularly Dr. Higgins. While they saw the ASI as a tool to be controlled and directed, she believed it was a partner in their quest for knowledge.

"Your grandfather was a brilliant man," Dr. Brennan said to Harvey, her voice tinged with respect and regret. "But he was afraid of what we were creating. He wanted to place limits on the ASI to constrain its growth and development. I argued we needed to let it evolve naturally. To trust in its ability to guide us towards a greater understanding of reality."

This philosophical divide had led to heated arguments and increasingly tense team meetings. Dr. Brennan's insistence on exploring the connection between the ASI and the unique properties of Ballynagowan was met with skepticism and resistance.

"They thought I was chasing fairy tales," she said, a hint of bitterness creeping into her voice. "They couldn't see the potential, the way the ASI could help us tap into the latent power that lay beneath our feet."

As the rift between Dr. Brennan and the rest of the team grew, her position became increasingly untenable. She spoke of late nights spent pouring over data, trying to find the proof she needed to convince her colleagues. But in the end, it wasn't enough.

"I was dismissed from the project," Dr. Brennan said, her voice heavy with the weight of the memory. "They said my ideas were too radical, too dangerous. That I was putting the entire endeavor at risk with my 'obsession' with Ballynagowan."

She paused, her eyes meeting Harvey's. "Your grandfather was the one who delivered the news. He said it was for the best, that my talents could be put to greater use elsewhere. But I knew the truth. They were afraid of what I represented, of the change I was trying to bring about."

Dr. Brennan's dismissal had been a turning point. Cut off from the resources and support of the ASI project, she had been forced to strike out on her own. She was pursuing her vision of a future where magic and technology were one.

"I founded QuantumCore," she said, gesturing to the gleaming facility around them. "I recruited brilliant minds who shared my passion, who believed in the potential of Reality Weaving. Together, we've achieved success which most scientists can only dream of."

"How does PulseWave Labs fit into all of this?" Harvey asked.

"QuantumCore purchased the assets of PulseWave Labs and many other similar companies, which had technology of interest to us," she stated.

"How could you have funded this project?" Cillian asked, a note of skepticism in his voice.

"I am fortunate to have several wealthy and powerful benefactors," she said dismissively.

She gestured at their surroundings. "This project, the Quantiforge, is the culmination of the ideas your grandfather rejected. Had he allowed me to pursue my ideas, the world would be a utopia of peace and happiness for all humanity." She paused. "But now, I fear my actions may have put everything at risk."

The team exchanged worried glances, their eyes reflecting shared confusion and unease. A heavy silence lingered in the air, amplifying the moment's tension. Harvey leaned forward slightly and asked cautiously, "What do you mean?" His voice carried a hint of urgency as if he sensed the gravity of the situation but was wary of what the answer might reveal.

Dr. Brennan's holographic controls flickered, showing a map of the world with pulsing red dots. "We're not the only ones who know about Ballynagowan's unique properties. There's another group, one with far less altruistic intentions, who seek to harness this power for themselves. We believe they've infiltrated our operation."

"Who are they?" Cillian asked, his voice barely above a whisper.

Dr. Brennan's expression darkened. "We're not entirely sure. But our intelligence suggests it's a rogue faction within a foreign government. Possibly with ties to international criminal organizations. They've been trying to weaponize reality manipulation technology for years."

Dr. Brennan was in the middle of her explanation when the insistent beeping of a device clipped to her lab coat broke the flow of her words. She paused, her brow furrowing in mild annoyance as she glanced down at the small screen. With an apologetic smile, she raised her hand to reassure the group. "I'm sorry, I need to attend to this, but I'll be back in a few minutes," she promised, her voice calm yet tinged with urgency.

The team exchanged worried glances as Dr. Brennan hurried out of the room, her abrupt departure leaving a palpable tension in the air. The sudden silence was oppressive, broken only by Ruffio's low whine of distress. The cyborg dog's ears were flat against his head, his advanced sensors clearly picking up on the unease permeating the room.

Maeve was the first to find her voice, her words tumbling out in a rush of nervous energy. "This is bad, right? I mean, really bad. QuantumCore isn't just pushing the boundaries of science; they're practically demolishing them. They're messing with the fundamental laws of physics, and I can't shake the feeling that they don't fully grasp the consequences."

She began pacing, her fingers flying over her tablet as she pulled up data from their earlier observations. "The energy readings we've been getting... they're off the charts. It's like nothing I've ever seen before. If they lose control of this technology, the results could be catastrophic."

Cillian nodded grimly. "My biggest concern is the shadowy nature of their funding. Who exactly is bankrolling this operation? It doesn't seem to align with any legitimate corporate or governmental research I'm aware of."

Harvey listened to his friends' concerns, feeling the weight of responsibility settle heavily on his shoulders. He wanted to reassure them and find some silver lining in this increasingly dire situation, but he couldn't shake his doubts.

"I hear you both," he said carefully, trying to keep his voice steady. "And I share your concerns. What troubles me most is Dr. Brennan's demeanor. Did you notice how she seemed almost... feverish with excitement? It's as if she's so caught up in the possibilities of their creation that she's blind to the potential dangers."

He ran a hand through his hair, a gesture of frustration. "I can't help but wonder if she truly understands the full scope of what they've created here. The way she talked about reshaping reality... it was like she saw it as a simple tool, not a force that could potentially unravel the very fabric of our existence."

Ruffio, sensing Harvey's distress, pressed against his leg comfortingly. Harvey heard the dog's synthesized voice through the earpiece, tinged with concern. "Detecting elevated stress levels in all team members. Recommend caution and further investigation before proceeding."

Harvey nodded, grateful for Ruffio's steady presence. "You're right, boy. We need more information before we can decide how to proceed."

The air in the room suddenly crackled with otherworldly energy, causing the hairs on the back of Harvey's neck to stand on end. Dr. Brennan materialized before them in a blinding flash of iridescent light, her lab coat billowing as if caught in an unseen wind. The team recoiled in shock, their eyes filled with awe and terror.

Dr. Brennan's eyes glowed with an unnatural, pulsing light. Her form seemed to flicker and waver as if she wasn't fully anchored in this reality.

Her face, which moments ago had been animated with enthusiasm, now bore a look of dawning horror. Her eyes darkened, and the color drained from her cheeks. She gripped the edge of a nearby console, her knuckles turning white.

"Doctor?" Harvey ventured cautiously, taking a step towards her. "Is everything alright?"

Dr. Brennan's gaze snapped to Harvey as if she'd forgotten they were there. She opened her mouth to speak, but no words came out. Instead, she turned sharply to a nearby display, her fingers typing across the keyboard with frantic urgency.

Maeve, her own tablet forgotten in her hands, watched Dr. Brennan's actions with growing concern. "What's happening?" she asked, her voice barely above a whisper.

A low, ominous hum began to fill the room. The lights flickered, and the air seemed to thicken, charged with an unseen energy.

"No, no, no," Dr. Brennan muttered, her voice echoing strangely as if coming from multiple places simultaneously. "This can't be happening. Not now. Not like this."

Cillian stepped forward. "Dr. Brennan," he said, his voice steady despite the fear evident in his eyes, "what exactly is going on here?"

She turned to face them, her expression full of fear. "It's the Quantiforge," she said, her words coming out in a rush. "Someone's trying to activate the core remotely. The security protocols... they're being overridden."

As if to punctuate her words, a series of alarms began to blare throughout the facility. The flashing red lights cast an intense, eerie glow across the worried faces of the team. The holographic displays flickered wildly, showing cascading error messages and security warnings.

"We need to stop this," Dr. Brennan continued, her earlier composure completely shattered. "If they gain full control of the Quantiforge... the consequences could be catastrophic."

"What's happening?" Maeve cried out, jumping to her feet. The table beneath them began to vibrate, its surface rippling like water.

"It's a breach, they are in the building!" Dr. Brennan screamed.

Ruffio's ears perked up, his whole body tensing. "I'm detecting a massive energy surge. It's exceeding all previous readings by a factor of ten!"

The room shuddered violently, and gravity seemed to fluctuate for a moment. Chairs, tablets, and even Cillian himself began floating toward the ceiling before crashing back down. The air in the room suddenly took on a life of its own. It was shimmering and undulating like a heat mirage but a hundred times more intense.

The team staggered as reality shifted around them. They watched in awe and fear as the Quantiforge's power manifested. Physics itself bent and warped. They found themselves at the center of a cosmic reshaping. The world they knew began to unravel, threatening to dissolve into chaos.

Harvey shuddered as understanding dawned. He stumbled, reality bending around the team. The implications of their situation sank in, filling him with dread. "The bakery incident, the drone in the park – they were tests, weren't they?

Whoever is behind this has been probing your defenses, and now..."

"Now they're making their move," Dr. Brennan finished grimly, her fingers holding onto the holographic controls, which were barely holding their form. "If they gain control of the Quantiforge, they could reshape reality on a global scale. Wars could be won by changing the laws of physics on a battlefield. Entire cities could be wiped from existence with a thought."

"You have to shut it down!" shrieked Maeve.

Dr. Brennan looked at her with a stern face, "No! It cannot be shut down. All my work will be lost forever!"

The room quaked again. Air churned and pulsed. Cracks split the walls. But these fissures revealed no concrete or metal. They offered glimpses of distant realms: a radiant beach, an icy tundra, a crowded alien metropolis. Reality crumbled around them, its boundaries dissolving.

"The dimensional barriers are collapsing!" Dr. Brennan shouted over the wailing alarms. "If we don't stop this soon, our reality could merge with countless others!"

Harvey scanned his friends' faces. Their expressions mirrored his own: a blend of resolve, fear, and wonder. They shared a silent moment of unity amid the chaos. "What can we do to help?"

Dr. Brennan managed a small smile despite the chaos. "I was hoping you'd ask. Your unique skills might be our best chance at stopping these individuals before they can cause irreparable harm."

She quickly moved to a control panel, her fingers typing over the holographic keyboard that kept trying to slip away from her touch. "I'm giving you access to our systems. We need to track down the infiltrators and stop them before they can fully activate the Quantiforge."

As sirens wailed and reality seemed to falter around them, Harvey felt a surge of adrenaline, unlike anything he'd experienced before. This was far beyond any mystery they had ever faced. But as he looked at his friends, he knew they were up for the challenge.

Harvey took a deep breath, meeting Dr. Brennan's gaze. " Tell us what we need to do," he said, his voice steady.

As Dr. Brennan began to outline their plan, the air in the conference room seemed to hum with a new intensity. The equations on the holographic displays swirled faster, and the energy patterns grew more complex. The very essence of reality seemed to shift in response to their unyielding determination. Their resolve to protect their world vibrated through the air, transforming their surroundings with an energy born of courage and hope.

And fight, they would. Because in the face of this new threat, there was no other choice.

As they sprang into action, the surrounding room shifted and warped. Glimpses of other worlds flickered in and out of existence, and the laws of physics seemed to be rewriting themselves with each passing second.

Harvey and his friends were the final defense against a potent, incomprehensible threat that could unravel their world. Driven by determination, they raced against time. To protect everything they cherished, fully aware of the immense stakes and challenges ahead.

Ruffio stood alert, his cybernetic eyes scanning the fluctuating environment for any sign of threat.

Suddenly, a violent tremor shook the facility. The floor beneath their feet rippled like water, and for a heart-stopping moment, gravity seemed to reverse. They clung to whatever they could grab, watching in terror as objects floated upwards before crashing back down.

Harvey caught a glimpse of another world through a crack that had appeared in one wall – a Ballynagowan that might have been or might yet be. The vision lasted only a second before the tear sealed itself, but it drove home the stakes of their mission.

Ruffio's ears twitched as he processed the data streaming through his advanced sensors. "Harvey, the anomalous activity is contained to this immediate area. No other chaotic atmospheres detected in the building. The Quantiforge's effects appear localized to this room only."

Harvey looked quizzically at Ruffio but didn't have time to process what he had said.

"We need to move now!" Dr. Brennan shouted, gesturing towards a door that hadn't been there moments before. "The Quantiforge chamber is this way – we must hurry!"

Without waiting for a response, she turned and bolted towards the door, which seemed to shimmer in and out of existence. Her lab coat billowed behind her like a cape, the fabric rippling strangely as it passed through areas of distorted space-time.

The group shared brief, knowing looks before dashing in pursuit of her retreating figure.

CHAPTER 11
REALITY UNHINGED

Alarms blared as Harvey, Ruffio, Maeve, and Cillian raced through the corridors of the underground complex. The air seemed to crackle and distort around them as reality itself protested against the unauthorized manipulation of the Quantiforge. The overhead lights flickered erratically, casting eerie shadows that danced along the walls, making it seem as if the physical structure of the facility was alive and writhing.

As they dashed through the chaos, Harvey shouted to Maeve, barely heard over the blaring alarms and their thundering footsteps. "Maeve, can you tap into the security systems of this facility?"

Maeve peered intently at her tablet, her face illuminated by the device's glow. Beads of sweat formed on her forehead as she fought against the rapidly deteriorating digital infrastructure of the complex. "I'm trying, but the interference is making it difficult. It's like the network itself is... shifting. Every time I think I've got a handle on it, the code mutates!"

As they rounded a corner, the group skidded to a halt.

Before them, the corridor split into three identical paths, each shimmering with a distinct hue. One bathed in an eerie red glow, another pulsing with a soft blue light, and the third crackling with green energy.

"Which way?" Cillian gasped, his glasses fogging up from the exertion.

Ruffio suddenly stopped, his ears twitching. His cybernetic eyes whirred as they recalibrated, scanning the environment. "Alert: Anomalous energy signatures detected ahead. Multiple quantum fluctuations are present. Extreme caution advised."

Suddenly, the corridor in front of them began to warp and twist, the walls melting like wax in a surrealist painting. The red path stretched impossibly long. The blue path started to curl in on itself like a Möbius strip. And the green path flickered in and out of existence.

"Look out!" Cillian cried, pulling Maeve back just as a portion of the floor beneath her feet vanished, revealing a swirling vortex of energy. The void pulsed with a hypnotic rhythm, threatening to draw them in.

Harvey's mind whirled frantically, adrenaline sharpening his thoughts. "The infiltrators must be using the Quantiforge to alter the complex's layout. They're trying to keep us from reaching the core."

"But how do we navigate if the structure of the building keeps changing?" Cillian asked, his voice filled with panic.

Harvey experienced a moment of inspiration. "Ruffio, your quantum entanglement with the AI core should be unaffected by these local reality distortions. Can you guide us?"

The cyborg dog's eyes glowed as he processed the request, lines of code reflecting in his irises. "Affirmative. Calculating optimal route now. Be advised: path will be hazardous. Recommend extreme caution."

Following Ruffio's lead, the team cautiously made their way through the shifting labyrinth of the complex. They chose the blue path, which seemed to stabilize momentarily under Ruffio's influence. As they progressed, the challenges grew increasingly surreal and dangerous.

They passed a room where gravity had reversed entirely. Office furniture floated near the ceiling, and loose papers swirled in a weightless dance. "Don't step in!" Harvey warned as Cillian nearly crossed the threshold. "We don't know if we'd be able to get back out!"

In another section, they encountered a corridor that looped back on itself in impossible ways. Every time they thought they'd made progress, they found themselves back where they started. Frustration mounted until Maeve had an idea.

"What if we walk backwards?" she suggested. "If the corridor is inverting our progress, moving in reverse might counteract it!"

To their amazement, it worked. Walking backward, they finally broke free of the loop, emerging into a new area of the facility.

As they pressed on, they entered a chamber where time seemed to flow backward. They watched in awe as shattered equipment reassembled itself and spilled liquids flowed back into their containers.

"Fascinating," Cillian murmured, furiously taking notes. "The Quantiforge isn't just affecting space, but time as well! The implications for historical research are—"

"Focus, Cillian!" Harvey interrupted, pulling his friend along. "We can discuss the academic consequences later if we survive this!"

As they neared the central chamber housing the

Quantiforge, Maeve suddenly gasped. "Guys, I've managed to access the security feeds partially. Look at this!"

She projected a holographic image from her tablet. It showed a group of figures in sleek, high-tech suits working at the Quantiforge controls. Their faces were obscured by helmets, but their movements were precise and deliberate. The central figure, taller than the rest, stood before a pulsing orb of energy. Their hands were outstretched as if conducting a silent orchestra of chaos.

"They're trying to control the Quantiforge," Maeve explained, her voice tight with concern. "If they succeed, the reality distortions could spread beyond Ballynagowan, maybe even globally. We're talking about a total breakdown of the laws of physics!"

The severity of the situation settled over the group like a heavy blanket. Harvey's expression hardened with determination, and his jaw set as he processed the immense responsibility they now faced.

"We can't let that happen," he said, his voice low but firm. "Cillian, what do you know about the layout of these old tech facilities? Any ideas on how we might be able to stop this?"

Cillian pushed his glasses up, thinking quickly. His eyes lit up as he recalled a crucial detail. "Well, most of them had emergency shutdown systems, usually accessible from multiple points for safety reasons. If we could find one of those terminals, we might be able to interrupt their process!"

"Good thinking," Harvey nodded, a glimmer of hope kindling in his chest. "Ruffio, can you locate the nearest emergency shutdown terminal?"

Ruffio's tail swished as he processed the request. His internal systems working overtime to filter through the chaotic data streams surrounding them. "Affirmative.

Emergency system shutdown console detected approximately 50 meters ahead. However, the path is highly unstable due to reality fluctuations. Conventional traversal may be impossible."

As they approached the area Ruffio indicated, they saw what he meant. The corridor ahead was a chaos of shifting matter and energy, sections disappearing and reappearing at random. Streams of data floated through the air like schools of digital fish. While pockets of alternate realities blossomed and withered in the blink of an eye.

"We'll never make it through that," Maeve said, her eyes narrowed as she scanned the turbulent space before them. "It's like trying to walk through a tornado made of broken physics!"

But Harvey wasn't ready to surrender quite yet. His mind pulsed with intensity, piecing together everything they'd learned about the Quantiforge and its effects. "Maybe we don't have to go through it physically. Ruffio, if Maeve boosts your signal, could you remotely interface with the emergency systems?"

Ruffio considered for a moment, his processors humming as they calculated the possibilities. "Possible, but it would require a significant power boost and a stable connection point. Current environmental interference exceeds my baseline capabilities."

Maeve grinned, catching on to Harvey's plan. Lines of code cascaded down the screen as she manipulated the tablet's operating system with swift, precise taps. "I can reroute power from my tablet to boost Ruffio's signal. But we'd need something to act as a focal point, to cut through all this quantum noise."

"Like this?" Cillian held up a small, innocuous-looking rock he'd picked up earlier at Aunt Eileen's cottage. In the chaotic environment, it seemed to glow faintly, pulsing in rhythm with the distant Quantiforge.

"A quantum entanglement stone!" Harvey exclaimed, recognizing it from their earlier encounter. "Cillian, you're a genius! That's exactly what we need!"

"I have my moments," Cillian replied with a modest smile, clearly pleased to have contributed.

"Perfect!" Harvey exclaimed, a plan forming in his mind. "Okay, team, let's do this. We don't have much time!"

With urgency and ingenuity, they established a makeshift command center in a relatively stable pocket of space. Maeve connected her tablet to Ruffio, rerouting power and amplifying his signal. Using a compass, Cillian carefully positioned the quantum stone.

Harvey kept watch, acutely aware that time was escaping them. The reality distortions were intensifying, and he could feel the fabric of space-time groaning under the strain. Sweat beaded on his forehead as he fought to maintain his focus amidst the chaos.

"Initiating emergency shutdown sequence," Ruffio announced, his eyes glowing brightly as he interfaced with the system. Streams of data flowed from the quantum stone, through Ruffio, and into the heart of the facility's systems.

For a tense moment, nothing seemed to happen. The group held their breath, the seconds stretching into what felt like an eternity. Then, suddenly, the chaotic energy fluctuations around them began to subside. The alarms quieted, and the air itself seemed to settle like a turbulent sea calming after a storm.

"It's working!" Maeve cheered, her eyes wide with disbelief and joy.

But their relief was short-lived. Just as they began to

celebrate their success, a deep, resonant hum began to build. The quantum stone started to vibrate intensely. Cracks appeared on its surface as it struggled to channel the immense energies flowing through it.

"Something's wrong," Harvey said, his instincts on high alert. A shudder of pure, unadulterated dread rippled through Harvey's body as he felt the air growing heavy with potential energy. "Ruffio, what's happening?"

The cyborg dog's ears flattened, a whine escaping him as his systems were bombarded with conflicting data. "Warning: Detected countermeasures activated. The infiltrators are attempting to override the shutdown. Quantiforge energy levels are approaching critical mass!"

The humming grew louder, drowning out all other sounds. The air around them began to ripple and distort, and cracks appeared in reality itself, golden light spilling through like sunbeams through storm clouds.

Cillian's eyes darted nervously around the chaotic scene before them. A whirlwind of hypotheses swirled through his consciousness, each grasping at the edges of rationality as he struggled to reconcile the fabric of reality with the surreal tapestry unraveling before his eyes.

"The shutdown," he began, his voice barely above a whisper. "It must have compromised their hold on the Quantiforge."

He paused, swallowing hard as the implications of his theory sank in. The surrounding air seemed to shimmer and twist, defying the laws of physics.

"This is unprecedented," Cillian continued, his words tumbling out faster now. "Reality itself is unraveling at the seams."

A sudden ripple in the air caused him to flinch. "The

barriers," he gasped, "the walls between dimensions—they're collapsing all around us!"

Through the widening cracks in reality, they caught glimpses of other worlds, other possibilities. In one, they saw a Ballynagowan consumed by a technological singularity, gleaming spires of impossible architecture reaching into an alien sky. In another, the town was a primordial forest, ancient megafauna roaming beneath the canopy of giant trees.

The quantum stone, overwhelmed by the conflicting energies, finally shattered. Shards of crystalline material exploded outward, narrowly missing the group as they ducked for cover. With the stone's destruction, the last remnants of stability vanished, and chaos truly began to reign.

Harvey looked at his friends, seeing the same fear and determination in their eyes. Despite the terrifying situation, he felt a surge of pride and affection for this brave, brilliant team. He knew they were all thinking the same thing: they had come too far to give up now.

"Alright, team," Harvey said, his voice steady despite the maelstrom of broken physics swirling around them. He stood tall, embodying a leadership that seemed to come from deep within him. "We've got one shot at this. The remote shutdown failed, so we need to get to the Quantiforge core and shut it down manually. It's going to be dangerous, and I won't lie – I don't know if we'll all make it back. But if we don't try, everything and everyone we know and love could cease to exist. Are you with me?"

Maeve stepped forward, her eyes blazing with determination. "Try to stop me, Higgins. Someone's got to keep you from doing anything too heroically stupid."

Cillian adjusted his glasses, a nervous but resolute smile on his face. "The chance to witness the reshaping of reality firsthand? Wild horses couldn't drag me away."

Ruffio padded to Harvey's side, pressing against his leg in a gesture of unwavering loyalty. "All systems committed to mission success, Harvey."

Harvey felt a lump in his throat, overwhelmed by the courage of his friends. "Then let's go save reality."

Venturing towards the heart of the Quantiforge, they found themselves amidst a surreal, chaotic landscape. The world around them twisted and morphed, shattering and reassembling in impossible forms. They vaulted over sudden chasms that yawned open beneath their feet, dodged swirling debris that orbited like tiny moons, and slipped through ghostly walls made ethereal and insubstantial.

Every step was a defiance of warped physics. Gravity shifted unpredictably. One moment, they waded through thick, molasses-like air. The next, they clutched desperately at anything anchored to avoid drifting into the void. Time itself stuttered and danced erratically. They relived moments or were hurled forward, skipping beats in the narrative of their journey.

Finally, battered but unbroken, they arrived at the massive doors leading to the Quantiforge core. The barriers pulsed with ghostly energy, simultaneously inviting and forbidding.

"This is it," Harvey said, looking at each of his friends in turn. "Whatever happens in there... I just want you all to know—"

"Save the speeches for after we've saved the world, Higgins," Maeve interrupted with a smirk, though her eyes shone with emotion.

"Indeed," Cillian added. "We've got a reality to fix, haven't we?"

Ruffio barked in agreement, the sound distorting strangely in the twisted air.

Harvey nodded, swallowing the lump in his throat. "Right then. Together?"

As one, they reached out and pushed open the massive doors, their hearts pounding with anticipation. The heavy panels swung open with surprising ease, and they stumbled forward, ready to face whatever chaos lay beyond.

But instead of the swirling vortex of energy they'd expected, they were met with... nothing.

The team froze in their tracks, staring in disbelief at the vast, empty chamber before them. The room was enormous, its high ceiling lost in shadows, its walls stretching out to form a perfect circle. But it was entirely, impossibly empty. No Quantiforge core, no swirling chaos, no sign of the reality-bending technology they'd been pursuing.

The silence was deafening after the chaos they'd experienced in the corridors. The air was still, almost unnaturally so, without even a hint of the energy distortions they'd grown accustomed to.

"What... what is this?" Maeve whispered, her voice echoing in the cavernous space. She tapped furiously at her tablet, brow furrowed in confusion. "All my readings just... flatlined. It's like we stepped into a dead zone."

Cillian spun in a slow circle, his mind struggling to make sense of the scene. "This can't be right. Where's all the equipment? The controls? There's not even a speck of dust on the floor!"

Harvey experienced a spine-tingling chill, a growing sense of unease settling in his stomach. "Ruffio," he said quietly, "what are you picking up?"

The cyborg dog's ears twitched, his sensors evaluating the

situation. When he spoke through Harvey's earpiece, his synthetic voice was laced with confusion. "Anomaly detected. Sensors indicate the Quantiforge is present in this room, occupying the entire space. However, visual and other sensory data contradict this data. Unable to reconcile conflicting information."

As the team exchanged bewildered glances, trying to process this impossible situation, a sound cut through the eerie silence. The soft click of a door closing echoed from the far side of the chamber.

Their heads snapped up in unison, eyes straining to see across the vast empty space. But there was no sign of movement, no hint of whoever – or whatever – might have just entered or exited the room.

Dread pooled in Harvey's stomach as his mind churned through a kaleidoscope of worst-case scenarios. The empty room, the contradictory sensor readings, the mysterious sound – none of it made sense. But one thing was clear: they had stepped into something far more complex and dangerous than they'd imagined.

"Stay alert," he whispered to his friends, his voice tense. "I have a feeling we're not alone in here, even if we can't see anyone. Whatever's going on, we need to be ready for anything."

As they cautiously began to move further into the room, their sense of being watched grew more substantial. The vast, empty chamber felt like a stage, and they felt like unwitting actors in a play they didn't understand.

In the shadows of the complex, a figure smiled behind their high-tech helmet, watching the group's approach on a holographic display.

"Impressive, Mr. Higgins," they murmured, fingers

switching between pulsating holograms, manipulating streams of radiant energy. "But the real test is yet to come. Let's see if you have what it takes to reshape destiny itself."

Harvey's footsteps echoed through the chamber as he guided his team forward. The air around them seemed to thicken with anticipation. As they progressed, subtle changes in their surroundings began to catch their attention.

Harvey noticed the lines between what should be possible and impossible were starting to blur. It wasn't dramatic or sudden but rather a gradual shift that made them question their perceptions. Science, imagination, and the flow of time were intertwined in ways they hadn't anticipated when they started this mission.

CHAPTER 12
TEMPORAL TEMPEST

Carefully, the team made their way out of the expansive, vacant chamber. The surroundings flickered and transformed, embodying an air of uncertainty and fluidity. The sterile walls and floors melted away, replaced by a scene so achingly familiar yet impossible that it took their breath away.

They found themselves standing in the heart of Ballynagowan, but not as they knew it. This was Ballynagowan of the past, a patchwork of memories and moments that held deep personal significance for each of them.

Harvey gasped as he recognized his grandfather's old study, exactly as it had been when he was a child. The air was thick with the scent of old books and pipe tobacco. In the worn leather armchair by the fireplace sat Dr. Finnian Higgins himself. Looking younger than Harvey had ever known him, his eyes twinkled with the same curiosity and warmth that had inspired Harvey's love for science.

Maeve's eyes filled with tears as she saw her vibrant and healthy grandmother tending to a garden that had long since been paved over in their time. The scene was infused with the golden light of a summer evening, and Maeve could almost feel the warmth of those forgotten days on her skin.

Cillian found himself face to face with his great-grandfather, a man he'd only known through faded photographs and family stories. The elderly man stood before an ancient standing stone. His gnarled hands traced the intricate carvings as he spoke in a low, melodious voice about the secrets of the past.

Even Ruffio seemed affected, his cybernetic systems momentarily overwhelmed by the flood of sensory data. Through Harvey's earpiece came a confused whine, followed by, "Detecting multiple temporal anomalies. Unable to distinguish between past and present."

As they moved forward, still reeling from the emotional impact of these impossible visions, the scenes shifted and blended. They walked through layers of memory and history, each step bringing them closer to people and places they had loved and lost.

Abruptly, the idyllic scenes faded, replaced by a more foreboding atmosphere. The chaos of the reality shifting facility returned with a vengeance.

As they rounded a corner, they found themselves face to face with three of the infiltrators in their sleek, high-tech suits. For a brief moment, both groups froze in surprise, the air thick with tension.

"Stop them!" one of the infiltrators shouted, raising a device that looked like a cross between a gun and a remote control.

Time seemed to slow as the device fired, a beam of shimmering energy heading straight for Harvey. But Ruffio was faster, leaping in front of his human friend. The beam struck the cyborg dog, and Ruffio's form seemed to flicker and distort for a heart-stopping moment.

"Ruffio!" Harvey cried out in anguish, his voice cracking with emotion. "Not him. Please, not him."

But Ruffio shook himself, his form stabilizing. "Systems recalibrating. Minimal damage was sustained. That was... unpleasant." The relief that flooded through Harvey was almost painful in its intensity.

Maeve took advantage of the infiltrators' surprise and tapped a command into her tablet. The lights in the corridor pulsated, and the infiltrators' suits powered down.

"EMP burst," Maeve explained with a grin. "Localized to their tech. Let's move!"

They raced past the now-immobilized infiltrators, Harvey pausing only to relieve them of their reality-altering devices. "These might come in handy," he said, tossing one each to Maeve and Cillian. The weight of the device in his hand was both reassuring and terrifying.

The team crept through the dimly lit corridor, their footsteps echoing against the metallic walls. Ruffio's sensors were on high alert, his cybernetic eyes scanning every shadow for potential threats.

Ruffio barked, "Alert...".

Bright lights flooded the hallway, momentarily blinding them. A commanding voice boomed through a loudspeaker, "Freeze! You're surrounded!"

Harvey's heart raced as he blinked rapidly, trying to adjust to the harsh glare. As his vision cleared, he saw masked figures in high-tech suits emerging from hidden panels in the walls, their weapons trained on the team.

"Seize them!" the voice ordered, its tone laced with malice. "And destroy the cyborg mutt!"

Chaos erupted in an instant. Maeve swung her tablet like a weapon, its edge connecting with an attacker's helmet. Cillian hurled his backpack at the nearest infiltrator. Harvey lunged to protect Ruffio, his body acting on instinct before his mind could fully process the danger.

Their efforts, though valiant, were futile against the overwhelming force. Outnumbered and outgunned, their adversaries moved with military precision.

Ruffio growled fiercely, positioning himself between Harvey and the attackers. His eyes glowed with a mix of tenacity and something almost human – fear.

"Ruffio, run!" Harvey shouted, his voice cracking. "Get out of here!" The cyborg dog hesitated, torn between his programming and his loyalty. "Go!" Harvey insisted, pushing him away. "Save yourself!"

In a blur of motion, Ruffio made his decision. He turned and bolted down the corridor, a streak of fur and metal. The infiltrators fired their weapons, energy beams scorching the walls where Ruffio had been moments before.

"After that abomination!" the disembodied voice commanded. Half the infiltrators peeled off, their footsteps thundering as they pursued the fleeing canine.

The remaining attackers subdued the team with brutal efficiency. Harvey struggled against his captor's iron grip, his muscles screaming in protest. "Where are you taking us?" Maeve demanded. Her voice was a combination of anger and fear.

A stony silence greeted their questions, amplifying the tension in the room.

Guards marched them through a dizzying maze of corridors, each turn further disorienting the group. Finally, they reached a steel door, which slid open with an ominous hiss. The captors stripped them of their possessions. Rough hands shoved the team unceremoniously inside, and the door locked behind them with a resounding click that seemed to echo their fate.

The room was small and bare, its cold, metallic walls offering no comfort or hope of escape. There were no windows or furniture – nothing but the harsh glare of overhead lights and the sound of their ragged breathing.

Harvey immediately tried to contact Ruffio through his earpiece, his fingers trembling as they pressed against the device. There was only static, a void where Ruffio's comforting presence should have been. His stomach dropped, a leaden weight of fear settling in its place.

"I can't reach Ruffio," he said, his voice shaking. "What if they... what if he's..." He couldn't bring himself to finish the thought.

Maeve placed a comforting hand on his shoulder, her touch grounding him in the moment. "Don't think like that," she said softly but firmly. "Ruffio's smart and tough. He'll be okay."

Cillian nodded in agreement, his glasses slightly askew from the scuffle. "She's right. We need to focus on getting out of here."

Harvey took a deep breath, forcing himself to push down his worry about Ruffio. "You're right," he said, his voice steadying. "We need a plan."

They began to examine their prison with meticulous care. The walls were smooth and seamless, offering no hint of weakness. The door had no visible handle or control panel on their side, its surface unbroken and unyielding.

Cillian ran his hands along the walls, his historian's instincts driving him to search for any hidden panels or weak spots. His efforts met with nothing but cold, unyielding metal.

"What about the ventilation system?" Harvey proposed, a note of desperation creeping into his voice. They looked up in unison, only to have their hopes dashed. The vent was tiny, barely big enough for a cat, let alone a person.

Time seemed to stretch endlessly as they tried everything they could think of. Nothing worked. With each failed attempt, their frustration grew, threatening to overwhelm them.

"We can't give up," Harvey said, though his voice lacked its usual conviction. "We have to stop whatever they're planning with the Quantiforge."

Maeve slumped against the wall, her usual energy drained by their circumstances. "But how?" she asked, her voice tinged with defeat. "We're trapped, and we don't even know what they're really up to."

Cillian paced the small room, his footsteps a restless rhythm. "There must be something we're missing," he muttered, more to himself than the others. "Some detail we've overlooked."

Harvey leaned in the corner of the room. "It's odd. This room isn't having any reality fluctuations. Ruffio mentioned to me that right before Dr. Brennan disappeared from the conference room, he wasn't detecting any other anomalies in the building. Just in that conference room."

Cillian and Maeve shot each other a look of pure confusion. Their eyes widening as they turned to face Harvey, trying to make sense of his bewildering statement.

Hours seemed to crawl by, each minute stretching into an eternity. They took turns resting and brainstorming. The constant hum of the facility's machinery was a maddening companion to their imprisonment.

Out of nowhere, chaos broke loose beyond their cell walls. The dull monotony shattered as muffled shouts and quick footsteps echoed like a gathering storm. The sharp zap of energy weapons cut through the noise, each burst growing louder and more urgent, setting their nerves on edge.

They pressed their ears to the door, straining to make sense of the commotion. The sounds of struggle intensified, drawing ever closer.

"What's going on out there?" Cillian murmured, his voice tinged with a hopeful yet wary edge, reflecting the swirl of emotions racing through him.

Before anyone could respond, a familiar bark cut through the din. Their hearts leaped in unison, a surge of hope flooding through them.

"Ruffio?" Harvey called out, hardly daring to believe it could be true.

The sounds of conflict reached a fever pitch, then abruptly ceased. Silence fell.

They held their breath, the moments stretching into an agonizing eternity. The tension hung heavy in the confined space, binding them in a shared, silent torment.

Without warning, the door slid open. There, standing proudly in the doorway, was Ruffio. His fur singed in places, one of his cybernetic legs sparking slightly. But his tail wagged happily at the sight of them, his canine face somehow managing to look both heroic and somewhat smug.

"Ruffio!" Harvey cried, flinging his arms around the cyborg dog. Tears of relief and joy streamed down his face. "Are you hurt? How did you...? We thought..."

Ruffio barked once, a sound of triumph and reassurance. The dog's synthesized voice came through Harvey's earpiece: "All systems functional. My bite is worse than my bark."

They laughed in relief and amazement, the tension of their captivity breaking like a dam. Maeve and Cillian joined the embrace, patting Ruffio affectionately and marveling at his resilience.

"You brilliant dog," Maeve said, grinning from ear to ear. "How did you manage to find us?"

Ruffio's eyes glowed as he processed the question, his response coming through clear and concise. "Infiltrated facility systems. Disabled security protocols. Took a bite out of crime."

Cillian shook his head in wonder, a smile playing on his lips. "Remind me never to underestimate you again, my friend."

Harvey looked out into the hallway, taking in the scene of their rescue. Unconscious guards lay scattered about, a testament to Ruffio's effectiveness. "We need to move quickly," he said, his voice filled with renewed determination. "Ruffio, can you guide us to the Quantiforge core?"

Ruffio barked an affirmative, his posture alert and ready. They quickly relieved the fallen guards of their weapons and communication devices, arming themselves for the challenges ahead.

"Let's finish this," Harvey said, his eyes shining with resolve. His friends nodded in agreement, their earlier despair replaced by a steely determination.

They began to move as a team when Maeve retreated the other way. She grabbed their backpacks and her tablet from a table near the subdued guards. "Can't leave these behind," she said.

They moved with a sense of urgency through the labyrinthine halls of the facility, their footsteps echoing against the cold, metallic floors. The sterile environment was a maze of intersecting corridors and starkly lit passageways, each turn potentially leading to unforeseen challenges.

Ruffio's sensors, attuned to the slightest variations in the environment, scanned continuously for any signs of danger. The team's breath hung in the air, mingling with the tension that gripped them as they followed Ruffio's lead. Every movement was coordinated. They trusted in Ruffio's abilities to steer them clear of harm.

Edging ever nearer to the Quantiforge core, Harvey's skin began to tingle as if a thousand tiny electric currents were dancing across his body. The hair on his arms stood on end, and he tasted something metallic on his tongue, like licking a battery. Each breath felt thick and heavy as if the air itself had become syrup.

Beside him, Maeve stumbled, her face contorting in discomfort. "My ears," she gasped, pressing her palms against the sides of her head. "It's like they're popping but won't stop!"

Cillian's glasses fogged up inexplicably, and he blinked rapidly, his eyes watering. "Everything's blurry," he muttered, "and not because of my glasses. It's like my vision can't decide what to focus on."

A wave of nausea hit Harvey, his stomach lurching as if he were on a rollercoaster. One moment, he felt as light as a feather; the next, it was as if an invisible weight was pressing down on his shoulders and threatening to drive him to his knees. His joints ached, bones seeming to creak and shift within his body.

Ruffio whined, his mechanical parts whirring erratically. The cyborg dog's fur stood on end, sparks occasionally jumping between the strands.

As they pushed forward, Harvey's perception of his own body began to warp. His limbs felt elongated one second and stubby the next. The ground beneath his feet alternated between feeling like quicksand and solid rock, making each step a challenge.

The team forged ahead, their bodies screaming in defiance against the sensory onslaught. Each step was a grueling clash with the warped tapestry of their world.

"We must be getting close," Maeve observed, her voice filled with trepidation. Her tablet, now functional again, beeped urgently. "These energy readings are amazing! Whatever they're doing with the Quantiforge, it's big."

They rounded a final corner, and a massive set of iron doors loomed before them. Intricate patterns of light pulsed across its surface, a hypnotic dance of energy and possibility.

"This has to be it," Cillian whispered, his voice barely audible over the thrumming power. "The Quantiforge core."

"How do we get in?" Maeve asked, eyeing the impenetrable-looking entrance. Her voice quivered slightly, betraying the fear they all felt.

Harvey studied the door for a moment. "Ruffio, can you interface with the locking mechanism?"

Ruffio stepped forward, a small panel opening in his side to reveal an array of connection ports. "Attempting interface now." Sparks flew as Ruffio connected, the cyborg dog's body trembling with the effort.

For a tense moment, nothing happened. Harvey held his breath, acutely aware of every second ticking by. "Come on, boy. You can do this".

Harvey took a deep breath, bracing himself for whatever lay beyond those doors. He looked at his friends and saw the same mix of fear and determination he felt mirrored in their eyes. Whatever's on the other side," he said solemnly, "we must be ready. Agreed?"

They nodded resolutely, a silent pact at that moment

moment. Ruffio pressed against Harvey's leg, a steady presence offering silent support.

The massive doors groaned open, a sound like the universe itself yawning. Blinding light spilled out, forcing them to shield their eyes.

As their vision adjusted, they stepped into the Quantiforge core. What they saw made them gasp in collective amazement and horror.

The scene that greeted them was both awe-inspiring and terrifying. The Quantiforge core was a massive, pulsating orb of energy, tendrils of light reaching out to touch every corner of the vast chamber. Around it, a dozen infiltrators toiled at various control stations, their movements urgent and focused. The air hummed with power, making Harvey's teeth ache and his hair stand on end.

At the center of it all stood a figure who exuded authority, their suit more elaborate than the others. A shiver cascaded down Harvey's spine as the figure turned to face the newcomers.

"Ah, young Mr. Higgins," the figure said, their voice distorted by their helmet but carrying a note of amusement. "I was wondering when you'd join us. I must say, I'm quite impressed you made it this far."

Harvey stepped forward, trying to project confidence he didn't entirely feel. His palms were sweaty, and he could hear his own heartbeat pounding in his ears. "Who are you? What are you trying to achieve here?"

The figure laughed manically, reaching up to raise their shield on the helmet.

A collective gasp tore through the team.

Faces drained of color, eyes widened in horrified recognition. The world narrowed to a pinpoint, and all focus was drawn to the face before them—a face that shattered everything they thought they knew.

The team stood frozen, suspended between denial and terrible comprehension. Their blood ran cold as recognition dawned. This single unveiled face had hurled them all into an abyss of uncertainty. Nothing would ever be the same.

It was Dr. Aoife Brennan.

CHAPTER 13

SHATTERED REALITY

Maeve recoiled, her lip curling in disgust. "You?" she shouted, her words filled with betrayal. "Why have you been lying to us?"

Dr. Brennan turned to face them, her eyes gleaming with an unnatural light. A manic smile passed across her lips, a stark contrast to the warm, mentoring presence they had known.

"Did you really think I'd entrust the most significant scientific breakthrough in human history to a group of children? You were extremely useful, I'll admit. Your actions helped us calibrate the final stage of the Quantiforge to its full potential."

"You lured us here and used us as guinea pigs?" Maeve shrieked.

"But why?" Cillian asked, his voice shaking. "You spoke about using this technology to help people!"

"Oh, we will help people," Dr. Brennan replied, her voice taking on a fervent edge. "By reshaping reality itself, we'll create a perfect world. No more disease, no more scarcity, no more limitations. We'll be gods!"

Harvey shook his head, his resolve hardening. The weight of responsibility settled on his shoulders, heavy but not unbearable. "You're messing with forces you can't control. You'll tear reality apart!"

"A small price to pay for perfection," Dr. Brennan said dismissively. She turned back to the Quantiforge, raising her hands. "And now, bear witness to the dawn of a new age!"

As the Quantiforge pulsed, Harvey felt his grip on sanity begin to slip. The world around him no longer made sense, and his mind struggled to process the impossible. A wave of vertigo struck him, not from physical movement but from the foundations of reality shifting beneath his feet.

Glimpses of alternate Ballynagowans flashed before his eyes, each one feeling as real and tangible as the next. A frantic drumbeat pounded in Harvey's chest., his breath coming in short gasps as his brain fought against cognitive dissonance. He saw himself in these other worlds—sometimes thriving, sometimes suffering—and the weight of infinite possibilities threatened to crush him.

Maeve's scream pierced through his mental fog, but it sounded distorted as if coming from both everywhere and nowhere at once. Harvey tried to reach for her to anchor himself in something familiar, but his own hand seemed foreign to him. A creeping sense of derealization set in; was he really here? Had he ever been real at all?

For a terrifying moment, Harvey felt his very identity beginning to fragment. Memories and personality traits flickering like faulty lightbulbs. The boundary between self and other, between reality and fiction, blurred into meaninglessness. In this instant, he understood with gut-wrenching clarity why the human mind wasn't meant to perceive reality in this way.

With a Herculean effort, Harvey forced himself to focus on one thought, one truth. He had to stop this, not only for Ballynagowan but for the sake of his own sanity and of everyone he loved.

Harvey looked at his friends, saw the determination in their eyes, and knew what they had to do.

"Maeve, can you regain access to the Quantiforge controls?" he asked quickly.

Maeve nodded, accessing her tablet. "I'm on it, but I'll need time!"

"Cillian," Harvey continued, "use what you know about the old legends. See if there's a connection between the druids' rituals and the Quantiforge technology."

As Cillian began poring over the historical data on a nearby console, Harvey turned to Ruffio.

"We need to keep them distracted. Ready for some teamwork, boy?"

Ruffio's tail wagged once, his eyes glowing with purpose. "Always, Harvey."

Together, Harvey and Ruffio began to move through the chamber. Harvey used the reality-altering devices they'd taken from the guards to create localized distortions. Platforms appeared and disappeared under the feet of Dr. Brennan's team, control panels shifted out of reach, and miniature gravity wells disrupted their movements.

Ruffio ran at lightning speed. He knocked over the guards and nipped at their ankles. His actions momentarily disrupting their work.

Dr. Brennan's face contorted with rage. "Stop them!" she commanded, but her team was in disarray, struggling against the chaotic environment Harvey and Ruffio had created.

"I've almost got it!" Maeve called out, her face illuminated by the glow of her tablet. "Just a few more seconds!"

But as her finger hovered over the final command, a tendril of energy lashed out from the Quantiforge, shattering her device. Maeve cried out in frustration and pain, clutching her burned hand, "My tablet! "

"No!" Harvey shouted, his heart sinking. "We were so close!"

Dr. Brennan's laughter sent a wave of unease through Harvey. "Did you honestly think it would be that simple? The Quantiforge protects itself. It desires this!"

Undeterred, Cillian called out, "Harvey! I think I've found something! The druids chanted specific frequencies to tap into the energy of the earth. If we can replicate those frequencies..."

"We might be able to stabilize the Quantiforge!" Maeve finished, her eyes lighting up despite the pain. "But how? My tablet's fried!"

Harvey's mind surged into overdrive, searching for a solution. His gaze fell on Ruffio, and an idea sparked. "Ruffio! Can you generate those frequencies?"

The cyborg dog's ears perked up. "Affirmative. Adjusting audio output now."

A low, rhythmic hum filled the air as Ruffio began to emit the ancient druidic frequencies. For a moment, it seemed to be working – the chaotic energy of the Quantiforge began to subside.

But then Dr. Brennan slammed her hand down on a control panel, and a wave of discordant energy washed over them. Ruffio yelped, his systems momentarily scrambled.

"Nice try," Dr. Brennan sneered. "But I've spent years studying this technology. You can't hope to match my understanding! Your idiot grandfather thought this was all nonsense, but look at me now!"

As Dr. Brennan's words hung in the air, their disparaging tone towards Harvey's grandfather ignited a fire within him. He felt a surge of anger course through his veins. The weight of his grandfather's legacy, the trust placed in him, and the fate of reality itself all converged in this crucial moment.

But then, as quickly as the rage had come, clarity washed over Harvey. His eyes smiled, a spark of inspiration illuminating them with newfound determination. At this moment, he realized they had been approaching this completely wrong. They weren't fighting against Dr. Brennan and her misguided ambitions. They were fighting for the vision his grandfather had believed in—a future where science and ethics worked hand in hand.

"Guys," Harvey called out, his voice cutting through the chaos of the Quantiforge chamber. "Gather round, quickly!"

Maeve, Cillian, and Ruffio converged on Harvey's position. They formed a tight circle amidst the swirling energies and chaotic realities. They could see the change in his demeanor, the set of his jaw that spoke of a plan forming.

With steady hands, Harvey reached into his pocket and pulled out the Quantum Harmonizer. The tiny, intricate device pulsed with a soft light. The swirling patterns seeming to dance in response to the wild energies surrounding them.

"Remember what my grandfather said," Harvey spoke quickly, his words charged with urgency and hope. "This isn't just a tool. It's a key to stabilizing quantum fluctuations. We've been trying to shut down the Quantiforge, but what if we can harmonize with it instead?"

Maeve's eyes lit up with understanding. "Of course! If we can sync the Harmonizer's frequencies with the Quantiforge..."

"We might be able to bring it under control without destroying it," Cillian finished, excitement overriding his fear.

Ruffio's sensors whirred as he processed the idea. "Probability of success: uncertain. But potential positive outcomes are significantly higher than the current course of action."

Harvey nodded, a smile tugging at his lips despite the gravity of the situation. "It's a long shot, but it's our best chance. We need to work together and focus our thoughts through the Harmonizer. Are you with me?"

His friends nodded without hesitation, their trust in Harvey absolute. As one, they placed their hands on the Quantum Harmonizer, forming a living circuit of determination and hope.

The device began to glow brighter, its patterns accelerating as if responding to their combined will. Harvey closed his eyes, focusing all his thoughts on harmony, balance, and the delicate interplay between science and ethics that his grandfather had championed.

The team stood united. With the Quantum Harmonizer pulsing in their grasp, they prepared to challenge Dr. Brennan's misguided vision with one of their own—a future where the power to shape reality was tempered by wisdom and compassion.

Harvey turned to face Dr. Brennan. "It's over, Doctor. You might understand the technology, but you've forgotten the most important thing – the human element. The connections that bind us that make reality worth preserving."

Dr. Brennan's face twisted with contempt. "Sentimental nonsense. I'll show you the true power of the Quantiforge!"

The team focused their collective will through the Quantum Harmonizer. The device began to emit a high-pitched whine, its glow intensifying with each passing second. The swirling patterns on its surface accelerated, blurring into a continuous stream of light that seemed to pulse in perfect counterpoint to the chaotic energies of the Quantiforge.

Dr. Brennan, realizing what they were attempting too late, lunged towards them. "No! You don't understand what you're doing!" she howled, her voice filled with desperation and fear.

But it was too late. With a sudden surge of power, the Quantum Harmonizer released a blinding burst of pure, white light. The energy expanded outward in a perfect sphere, washing over everything in its path.

In that crucial moment, Ruffio sprang into action. The cyborg dog's body expanded and shifted, panels opening across his frame to create a shimmering energy shield that enveloped Harvey and his friends. The team huddled together, protected by Ruffio's advanced technology, as the wave of energy passed over them.

The light engulfed Dr. Brennan and her team. Without protection, they were thrown backward, collapsing to the ground unconscious as the energy overloaded their systems.

As quickly as it had begun, the burst of light faded. The wild, reality-warping energies that had filled the chamber moments before began to subside. The Quantiforge, which had been a maelstrom of uncontrolled power, settled into a steady, quiet hum. Its core still glowed, but now it was a smooth, pulsing light that seemed almost peaceful.

Ruffio's shield flickered and faded as the danger passed. Harvey and his friends slowly straightened up, looking around in awe at the transformed chamber.

"Did we... did we do it?" asked Cillian.

Maeve consulted one of the terminals, her eyes reading the data. "Energy levels are stabilizing. The reality distortions are collapsing back in on themselves. I think... I think we actually did it!"

The enormity of what they had accomplished began to sink in. Time and again, they had stared into the abyss of unreality, witnessing horrors that defied comprehension and challenged the foundations of their sanity. Yet somehow, against all reason and expectation, they had persevered through sheer determination, ingenuity, and no small amount of luck.

Harvey felt a wave of exhaustion wash over him as the adrenaline began to fade. He looked at each of his friends in turn, seeing the same mix of fatigue and disbelief on their faces.

"We did," he said softly, a smile tugging at his lips. "We really did it."

Unable to contain themselves any longer, the team burst into relieved laughter. They hugged each other tightly, the Quantum Harmonizer still clutched in Harvey's hand, pulsing warmly as if sharing in their joy.

Ruffio nuzzled Harvey's hand, his tail wagging weakly. "Mission accomplished," he reported through the earpiece, his synthesized voice somehow conveying both pride and exhaustion. "Recommend immediate rest and system diagnostics."

The now-quiet hum of the stabilized Quantiforge surrounded them. Harvey couldn't help but feel a sense of profound change. They had saved Ballynagowan – perhaps the entire world – from a threat beyond imagination.

Now, standing in the aftermath of their final victory, they realized the true power had never been in the reality-warping tech. It was in the bonds they'd forged, tempered by adversity and strengthened by choice. Their trust in one another, their willingness to sacrifice for each other, and their ability to find light even in the darkest moments—this was the real magic.

They had rewritten the rules of reality itself, not with equations or machines, but with the simple, unbreakable power of their friendship.

CHAPTER 14

GUARDIANS OF REALITY

The cool night air hit Harvey's face as he stepped out of the building that housed the Quantiforge. It was a welcome contrast to the charged atmosphere they'd left behind. Maeve, Cillian, and Ruffio followed close behind, their footsteps echoing in the eerie quiet of the abandoned tech park. The adrenaline that had fueled them through their confrontation with Dr. Brennan was beginning to ebb, leaving them exhausted but exhilarated.

As they made their way down the cracked concrete path, the reality of what they'd accomplished began to sink in. They had faced impossible odds, stared down the barrel of reality-warping technology, and emerged triumphant. The weight of their achievement hung in the air between them, almost too enormous to comprehend.

Cillian was the first to break the silence, his voice full of relief and uncertainty. "So... what do we do now? Should we call the authorities?"

Before anyone could respond, a gruff voice cut through the darkness. "We are the authorities."

The team came to an abrupt halt, instinctively huddling together for safety. Ruffio's ears perked up, his sensors whirring as they scanned the surroundings. In an instant, powerful floodlights flared, dispelling the darkness and illuminating everything with a blinding intensity. Harvey shielded his eyes from the sudden glare. His vision gradually acclimated to the scene unfolding before him, leaving him momentarily breathless.

Encircling them were countless military personnel, a formidable presence that spoke of authority and control. Official vehicles were strategically positioned in a broad perimeter. Their lights cast an eerie, surreal glow across the overgrown landscape of the tech park.

A towering figure stood at the heart of this orchestrated spectacle, his posture exuding command. The insignia on his uniform clearly indicated his rank and the pivotal role he played in this operation. The air was thick with tension and unasked questions, each passing second amplifying the gravity of the situation.

The commander stepped forward. His stern expression softened slightly as he took in the group of exhausted teenagers and one cyborg dog before him. "At ease, kids. We're here to help."

Maeve found her voice first, stepping forward with relief and wariness. "Who... who are you? How did you know to come here?"

The commander's lips quirked in what might have been a smile. "Colonel James McIntosh, Irish Defense Forces, Army Ranger Wing at your service. As for how we knew..." He paused, his eyes twinkling with amusement. "Let's just say we got a call from an old friend. One Eileen Higgins, to be precise."

At the mention of Aunt Eileen, the tension drained from

Harvey's shoulders. A huge smile came across his face. Of course, she'd been looking out for them, even from afar. He should have known she wouldn't send them into danger without a safety net.

Maeve let out a laugh that was half relief, half hysteria. "Auntie called in the cavalry. Of course, she did."

The Colonel nodded, his expression growing serious once more. "Now, I think it's time you filled us in on exactly what happened in there. From the energy readings we've been getting, it seems like you've had quite the adventure."

The next hour passed in a blur of activity. Medical personnel swarmed around them, checking for injuries. Technicians hurried in and out of the building behind them. Through it all, the team recounted their harrowing experience. They spoke in fits and starts, piecing together the fragments of their ordeal. They told of Dr. Brennan's betrayal, the reality-warping effects of the Quantiforge, and their desperate gambit with the Quantum Harmonizer. Throughout it all, the Colonel listened intently, his eyebrows rising higher with each incredible detail.

When they finished, Colonel McIntosh let out a low whistle. "Well, I've got to hand it to you kids. You've just saved us from a disaster of unprecedented proportions. I'm not sure many grown adults would have handled themselves half as well in your situation."

Harvey felt a flush of pride at the Colonel's words, but it was quickly tempered by the enormity of what they'd been through. "What happens now?" he asked, glancing back at the tech buildings. "With Dr. Brennan, and the Quantiforge, and... well, everything?"

The Colonel's expression turned grim. "Dr. Brennan and

her team will be taken into custody. As for the Quantiforge... that's above my pay grade. But I can assure you it will be handled with the utmost care and security."

He paused, looking each of them in the eye. "What you've done here tonight... it's going to have far-reaching consequences. There will be debriefings and investigations, but for now, I think what you all need most is rest."

With a gesture, the Colonel summoned several military personnel. "These fine folks will escort each of you to your homes. Get some sleep – you've more than earned it. We'll meet again at your Aunt Eileen's place in eight hours, at 10 AM sharp. There's still much to discuss."

As the team prepared to part ways, they found themselves reluctant to separate. The bond forged through their shared ordeal felt almost tangible, a thread connecting them that they were reluctant to break.

Maeve was the first to move, pulling Harvey and Cillian into a fierce hug. "We did it," she whispered, her voice thick with emotion. "We actually did it."

Cillian nodded, his glasses slightly askew from the embrace. "I still can't quite believe it. We saved reality itself."

Harvey felt a lump form in his throat as he held his friends close. "Thank you," he said softly. "I couldn't have done this without you. Any of you." He looked down at Ruffio, who wagged his tail in response.

As they broke apart, wiping away tears they'd pretend not to notice later, Harvey felt a surge of gratitude for these incredible people in his life. They had faced the impossible together and come out stronger for it.

The ride home was a blur of streetlights and quiet reflection. The night's revelations cascaded through Harvey's thoughts, but exhaustion quickly overtook him. By the time the military vehicle pulled up to his house, he was struggling to keep his eyes open. It was now 2:15 AM.

As he trudged up the path to his front door, Ruffio was a comforting presence at his side. Harvey couldn't help but think of his grandfather. He wondered what Dr. Finnian Higgins would have thought of their adventure, of the way they'd used his invention to save the day.

Entering his room, Harvey's gaze fell on a photograph on his bedside table. It showed him as a young boy, sitting on his grandfather's lap in the study, both grinning at the camera. He picked it up, running his thumb over the image.

"We did it, Grandpa," he murmured. "We protected your legacy. I hope... I hope you'd be proud."

As Harvey crawled into bed, Ruffio curling up at his feet, he felt a deep sense of satisfaction settle over him. They had faced an incredible challenge and risen to meet it. Whatever came next, he knew they'd face it together.

With that comforting thought, Harvey drifted off to sleep. The Quantum Harmonizer pulsing softly on his nightstand was a quiet reminder of the extraordinary adventure they'd just lived through.

Harvey was roused from a deep sleep in the morning by a warm, wet sensation on his face. He groaned, trying to turn away, but the persistent licking continued. Finally, he cracked open an eye to see Ruffio standing over him, tail wagging.

"Alright, alright, I'm up," Harvey mumbled, reaching out to scratch behind Ruffio's ears. As he did so, his eyes fell on the clock, and he bolted upright. "9:30? Oh no, we're going to be late!"

Ruffio spoke through Harvey's earpiece. "No anomalous events to report. All systems operational."

In a whirlwind of activity, Harvey rushed through his morning routine. Scarfing down a quick breakfast as he tried to tame his unruly hair. Ruffio watched with amusement. His head tilted to one side as Harvey hopped around, trying to pull on his shoes and grab his backpack at the same time.

They made it to Aunt Eileen's cottage with just minutes to spare. As Harvey burst through the door, slightly out of breath, he was greeted by the sight of Maeve and Cillian already seated at the kitchen table, steaming mugs of tea in front of them.

"Look who finally decided to join us," Maeve teased, but her smile was warm.

Before Harvey could retort, he was enveloped in a fierce hug. Aunt Eileen held him tight, and when she pulled back, her eyes were shining with unshed tears.

"Oh, Harvey," she said, her voice thick with emotion. "Your grandfather would be so proud of what you've accomplished. All of you," she added, looking around at the group.

Harvey's chest tightened, an invisible vise squeezing his heart as her words sank in. He'd been so caught up in the adventure, in the immediate danger, that he hadn't fully processed how his actions might have honored his grandfather's legacy.

Sensing the need to lighten the mood, Cillian piped up with a grin. "Well, my parents say I can't play with Harvey anymore. Apparently, saving reality from collapse is a bit too much excitement for their liking."

Maeve snorted into her tea. "That's nothing. My mom informed me that not only am I grounded, but my future great-grandchildren are also preemptively grounded. Talk about long-term punishment!"

Their laughter was interrupted by a knock at the door. Colonel McIntosh entered, followed by several official-looking individuals in suits. The mood in the room immediately sobered.

Over the next few hours, the government officials debriefed the team. They recounted their adventure in painstaking detail, from their first encounter with the strange phenomena in town to their final confrontation with Dr. Brennan. The officials listened intently, occasionally interjecting with questions or requests for clarification.

When they had finished, one of the officials, a stern-looking woman with graying hair, leaned forward. "I want you all to understand the magnitude of what you've accomplished," she said, her voice carrying a note of genuine admiration. "Your actions may very well have saved not just Ballynagowan or Ireland but potentially the entire world from a catastrophe we can scarcely imagine. You've done an extraordinary job."

The team's eyes flicked from face to face, showing a combination of pride and disbelief. It was one thing to know they'd done something important but to hear government officials state it so plainly made it feel suddenly, overwhelmingly real.

As the debriefing concluded and the officials prepared to leave, Colonel McIntosh turned to them one last time. "Remember," he said, his voice low and serious, "much of what we've discussed here today is classified. The world isn't ready to know the full extent of what happened. Can we trust you to keep this to yourselves?"

The team nodded solemnly, understanding the responsibility they were being given. Even Ruffio issued an affirmative bark.

As Colonel McIntosh was leaving, he turned to Aunt Eileen, presented a salute, and said, "Thank you, General Higgins."

Harvey gasped, "General!"

Aunt Eileen gave a wink with a twinkle in her eye.

After the officials had gone, Aunt Eileen brought out a veritable feast for lunch. As they ate, the mood gradually lightened, and soon, they were recounting their adventure with excitement and laughter.

Harvey laughed along with his friends, feeling a warm glow of contentment. He caught Aunt Eileen's eye and saw her beaming at them all, pride radiating from her entire being.

Suddenly, the front door burst open. Harvey leaped to his feet, his heart pounding as he recognized the figures standing in the doorway.

"Mom? Dad?" he gasped, scarcely believing his eyes.

His parents rushed forward, wrapping him in a warm, tight hug. The world fell away for a moment, and Harvey was simply a boy reunited with his family after far too long apart.

When they finally pulled back, Harvey turned to Aunt Eileen, who was watching the scene with a satisfied smile. "You did this?" he asked, his voice emotional.

Aunt Eileen shrugged, her eyes twinkling. "I told you I was going to make some phone calls, didn't I?"

As his parents began to fuss over him, asking a million questions and marveling at how much he had grown, Harvey caught sight of Ruffio. The cyborg dog was sitting quietly in the corner. Contentedly chewing on a biscuit, his glowing eyes taking in every detail of the joyful reunion. And in those eyes, Harvey swore he could see his grandfather looking back at him.

In that moment, Harvey stood surrounded by his friends, family, and the loyal companion who had been by his side through everything. A profound happiness washed over him, so intense it was almost overwhelming. Together, they had faced unimaginable challenges and stared down the very fabric of reality itself. Yet, they emerged not only victorious but also stronger and closer than ever before.

As the chatter and laughter filled the room, Harvey knew whatever adventures lay ahead, they would face them together. And that, he realized, was the greatest victory of all.

CHAPTER 15
BOUNDLESS HORIZONS

In the days after the Quantiforge adventure, Harvey and Ruffio found themselves whisked away to Dublin. They accompanied Harvey's parents to the Global Ethics Network Headquarters. Harvey cherished this unexpected opportunity to spend quality time with his parents. They shared meals together, savoring the local cuisine. They explored the vibrant city, discovering its hidden gems. Long conversations filled their evenings, where Harvey recounted his adventures and listened intently to his parents' work in AI ethics. These moments brought them closer, deepening their understanding of each other's worlds.

During their stay, Ruffio underwent a series of repairs and upgrades at the Global Ethics Network's advanced facilities. The experience had left the cyborg dog even more capable than before, though the specifics of his enhancements were kept strictly confidential. One notable change, however, was Ruffio's new ability to communicate directly with Maeve and Cillian. A feature that Harvey knew would prove invaluable in their future adventures. Yet, for the wider world not yet ready to accept a talking dog, Harvey would still need to wear his earpiece to hear Ruffio when others were around.

As much as Harvey had enjoyed his time in Dublin and the closeness with his parents, he found himself increasingly eager to return to Ballynagowan. The quaint town, with its hidden wonders and the friends who had stood by him through the most extraordinary of circumstances, called to him.

Today, the noon sun cast a warm, golden glow over Ballynagowan, its rays filtering through the vibrant foliage of Willow Creek Park. Harvey sat on a weathered wooden bench, his fingers absently tracing the grain of the armrest. Ruffio lounged contentedly at his feet, occasionally lifting his head to sniff the crisp air.

Ten weeks had passed since the Quantiforge incident. Life in the town had mostly settled back into its usual rhythm—or as normal as Ballynagowan ever managed to be. The park was alive with activity, a testament to the town's resilience. Children filled the air with laughter as they chased each other around the playground. Nearby, joggers and bicyclists navigated the winding paths, enjoying the fresh air and sunshine. Families gathered for picnics, spreading blankets on the grass and sharing stories. Despite the recent upheaval, the community's spirit remained unbroken, thriving in the heart of Ballynagowan.

Harvey closed his eyes, letting the sun's gentle warmth wash over him. He inhaled deeply, savoring the scent of fallen leaves and distant wood smoke. The events of that fateful day still felt surreal, like a vivid dream that refused to fade upon waking.

"Penny for your thoughts?" came a familiar voice, tinged with a lilting Irish accent.

Harvey looked up to see Maeve approaching, her flame-red

hair catching the sunlight. She carried her new tablet, but today, it was accompanied by a steaming thermos and three mugs.

"Just reflecting," Harvey replied with a warm smile.

She leaned down and hugged him tightly. "So glad you are back," Maeve whispered.

Maeve patted Ruffio on the head and then sat next to Harvey. "It's hard to believe everything that's happened."

Ruffio's ears perked up as Cillian joined them, his arms laden with books and what appeared to be an ancient scroll. "I hope I'm not late," Cillian said, slightly out of breath. "I got caught up researching some new theories about the druids' connection to quantum mechanics. You wouldn't believe the correlations I've found between their stone circles and the Quantiforge's energy patterns!"

Harvey chuckled, shaking his head fondly. "Glad to see you too! You're right on time, Cillian. Though I think we might need a translator for whatever you've just said."

Maeve grinned, pouring steaming tea into the mugs and passing them around. "I've got just the thing. Nothing beats a good cuppa for making sense of the impossible."

As they settled in, sipping their tea, Harvey leaned forward, his expression growing serious. "Now that we're all here, what's the latest update? How's Ballynagowan faring?"

Maeve's fingers slid across her tablet, pulling up various reports and charts. "Well, the good news is that reality has fully stabilized. No more bread turning into rocks or gravity going haywire."

"And the Quantiforge?" Harvey asked, his brow furrowing with concern.

"Safely put into standby mode and under 24/7 guard," Maeve confirmed, her voice carrying a note of relief. "The government has a team of scientists studying it, trying to understand its technology without risking another incident. They've set up a research facility in the old tech park. It's nice to see it come back to life after all these years."

Harvey nodded, taking a thoughtful sip of his tea. The warm liquid seemed to chase away the chill of memory. "I suppose we should be grateful for their interest. Better than leaving it to gather dust—or worse, fall into the wrong hands."

Cillian pushed his glasses up, his eyes shining with excitement. "Speaking of hands, you wouldn't believe what the historical society has uncovered! All those glimpses of the past we saw during the reality fluctuations? They've opened up entirely new avenues of research into Ballynagowan's history."

He unfurled the scroll he'd been carrying, revealing intricate diagrams and ancient Celtic script. "The librarians are allowing me to study this scroll. It was recently discovered in the library's archives. It details a series of ley lines converging exactly where the Quantiforge core appeared. The druids knew, guys. They knew something like this could happen, even centuries ago!"

Maeve leaned in, examining the scroll with interest. "That's fascinating, Cillian. But how does it connect to your quantum mechanics theory?"

As Cillian launched into an enthusiastic explanation, Harvey's mind wandered to another pressing concern. "And what about Dr. Brennan?" he asked, interrupting Cillian's scientific musing. "Any word on her fate?"

A shadow passed over Maeve's face as she set down her mug. "She's still in custody. The authorities have finally reached a decision. Given the unprecedented nature of her actions, they've opted for a unique approach. Dr. Brennan will be placed under house arrest, but she'll be allowed to continue her research under strict supervision from the Global Ethics Network. They're hoping her brilliance can be channeled into more... constructive pursuits."

Harvey frowned, conflicting emotions portrayed across his face. "She was brilliant in her own way. Misguided, certainly, but... I can't help but wonder if we could have prevented this if she had been willing to work with my grandfather's team sooner."

Cillian placed a comforting hand on Harvey's shoulder. "We can't change the past, my friend. What matters is how we move forward. And speaking of moving forward, I've got some news of my own."

Harvey and Maeve turned to him, giving him their full attention. Cillian's face broke into a wide grin. "The library has offered me a position as a visiting lecturer. They want me to teach a course on 'Quantum Anomalies and Historical Intersections.' Can you believe it?"

"Cillian, that's wonderful!" Maeve exclaimed while Harvey reached over to shake his hand firmly.

"Congratulations, old friend," Harvey said warmly. "They couldn't have chosen a nicer person for the job."

Maeve's tablet chimed, drawing their attention. "And it looks like my news is officially confirmed, too," she said, her eyes scanning the screen. "The town council has approved my proposal for a new department: Anomalous Event Management and Research. We'll be working closely with the scientific team at the tech park, but our focus will be on helping the town prepare for... well, whatever might come next."

Harvey sat back, a sense of pride and contentment washing over him. "Look at you two," he said softly. "Ballynagowan's very own dynamic duo of the strange and unusual."

"Trio," Maeve corrected, nudging him gently. "Don't think you're getting out of this, Harvey Higgins. We'll need your level head and years of experience to keep us grounded."

Harvey laughed, raising his mug in a toast. "To new beginnings, then. Also, to Ballynagowan -- may it never lose its capacity to surprise us."

A comfortable silence fell over the group as they clinked their mugs together. The afternoon sun began its descent towards the horizon, painting the sky in brilliant oranges and purples. Children were called home for dinner, and the park slowly emptied, leaving the three friends to their thoughts.

Unexpectedly, Cillian burst into laughter, his shoulders shaking as he tried to contain his glee. Harvey and Maeve exchanged puzzled glances, their eyebrows raised in silent question.

"What's so funny?" Maeve asked, a hint of amusement in her voice.

Wiping tears from his eyes, Cillian managed to catch his breath. "I just realized," he chuckled, "school starts again tomorrow. I can't wait for Miss Wormwood to assign her 'What I Did On My Summer Vacation' essay."

The absurdity of the situation hit them all at once, and soon they were all laughing. Harvey, between fits of giggles, quipped, "Oh yeah, I can see it now: 'This summer, I saved reality from collapsing and prevented an evil scientist from becoming a god. Also, I walked my dog.'"

Maeve snorted, adding, "Don't forget the part where we decoded ancient druid magic and quantum physics. That's sure to get us extra credit!"

Ruffio, catching the infectious mood, wagged his tail and let out a playful bark.

As their laughter subsided, Cillian sighed contentedly.

"You know, sometimes I think Miss Wormwood assigns this essay just to see who can come up with the most creative lies. This year, the truth might be stranger than fiction!"

"So," Harvey said, breaking the comfortable silence that had settled over the group, "I've been thinking about my parents and their plans."

Maeve and Cillian exchanged glances. Harvey's parents, international ambassadors for AI ethics, had been a sensitive topic since their extended absence began years ago. But it had evolved significantly during their recent time together in Dublin.

"What's on your mind?" Maeve asked gently, sensing the thoughtful tone in Harvey's voice.

Harvey nodded, his face becoming emotional. "They're going to be coming back to Ballynagowan more frequently. Not permanently, but they want to spend more time here. I think everything that's happened has made them realize how much they've missed."

"That's wonderful news!" Cillian exclaimed, then paused, noticing the complex expression on Harvey's face. "Isn't it?"

"It is," Harvey assured him, a small smile forming. "It's just... I've realized how much I've grown while they've been away. Being with them in Dublin was wonderful, but it also showed me how much has changed."

"You're worried about finding a new balance," Maeve suggested, her voice soft with understanding.

Harvey sighed, running a hand through his hair. "Exactly. We've been through so much together," he gestured to his friends and Ruffio, "and they've missed a lot of it. I want them to be part of my life here, but I also don't want to lose the independence I've gained."

"It's natural to feel this way," Cillian said thoughtfully.

"But remember, they're coming back because they want to be part of your life. They're probably just as nervous about fitting in as you are about having them around more."

Maeve nodded in agreement. "And don't forget, you're not the same kid they left behind. You've faced reality-bending psychopaths and saved the world. I think you can handle navigating a changing family dynamic."

Harvey smiled at his friends. "You're right. It's just another adventure, isn't it? Balancing family, friends, and whatever weirdness this town throws at us next."

"Exactly," Cillian grinned. "And hey, maybe having your parents around more often will come in handy. We could use some expert advice on AI ethics the next time we're facing down a rogue quantum computer."

The group laughed, the mood lightening. Harvey felt a warmth spread through his chest as he looked at his friends. They had faced the impossible together, and this new chapter in his life was just another challenge they'd tackle as a team.

"Thanks, guys," Harvey said sincerely. "I'm glad you'll be with me through this too."

A low growl from Ruffio startled the group, instantly silencing their lighthearted conversation. The cyborg dog's ears perked up, his body tensing as his advanced sensors detected an approaching presence.

"What is it, boy?" Harvey whispered. His hand resting on Ruffio's back. The dog's growl deepened, his cybernetic eyes glowing and fixed on the park's edge.

A moment later, a familiar figure came into view – Dr. Aoife Brennan, accompanied by two stern-looking government agents.

The trio fell silent as Dr. Brennan approached. She looked older than when they'd last seen her, the stress of recent months etched into the lines of her face. Yet there was a fire in her eyes that hadn't dimmed.

"Mr. Higgins," she said, her voice carrying a hint of its old authority. "Miss Murphy, Mr. O'Brien. I hope I'm not interrupting."

Harvey stood, his posture tense but not hostile. "Dr. Brennan. This is... unexpected."

She nodded, a wry smile appearing. "I'm sure it is. I've been granted permission to speak with you before I begin my... rehabilitation." She glanced at the agents, who maintained a respectful distance. "I wanted to apologize. My actions were inexcusable, driven by hubris and a misguided notion of progress."

Harvey studied her for a moment, searching for any sign of deception. Finding none, he relaxed slightly. "Thank you, Dr. Brennan. That... means a lot."

"I also wanted to thank you," she continued, her voice growing softer. "You showed me that the true power of the Quantiforge – of any great discovery – lies not in control but in understanding. In cooperation."

Maeve and Cillian had risen to stand beside Harvey, presenting a united front. Maeve spoke up, her tone cautious but not unkind. "And what will you do now?"

Dr. Brennan's eyes lit up with a familiar spark of enthusiasm. "I've been given the opportunity to continue my research, under strict guidelines, of course. But instead of trying to manipulate reality, I'll be focusing on how we can better understand and protect it. Your actions during the crisis have not gone unnoticed. They've opened up entirely new avenues of study."

As Dr. Brennan shared some of her new theories, Harvey found himself drawn into the discussion despite his initial reservations. The scientist's passion for knowledge was genuinely infectious. Before long, all four of them engaged in a lively debate. They discussed the nature of reality, delving into its complexities. The conversation touched on the responsibilities that come with understanding such profound concepts.

Long shadows crept across the park as the sun dipped below the horizon. Dr. Brennan's handlers signaled it was time to leave. She bid them farewell, pausing to address Harvey one last time.

"Mr. Higgins," she said. Her voice carried a note of respect that hadn't been there before. "You and your friends have a remarkable gift. You see the wonder in the world, the potential for discovery, without losing sight of what truly matters. Don't ever lose this."

With that, she turned and walked away, leaving the trio to ponder her words.

As darkness fell, the park came alive with an ethereal glow. Tiny points of light, remnants of the Quantiforge's energy, drifted through the air like fireflies. It was a reminder of how thin the veil between worlds had become and of the responsibility they now carried.

"Well," Maeve said, breaking the contemplative silence, "I don't know about you two, but I could use a proper meal after all this heavy talk. O'Malley's Pub?"

Harvey grinned, feeling the emotional weight of the day lifting from his shoulders. "Sounds perfect. I hear they've finally managed to update their menu – no more dishes accidentally summoned from the 18th century."

Harvey took one last look around the park as they gathered their things and prepared to leave. The drifting lights, the ancient trees, the modern buildings in the distance. All of it was a testament to Ballynagowan's unique blend of past and future, science and magic.

"You know," he said thoughtfully, "when I was younger, I used to dream about having grand adventures, about making a difference in the world. I never imagined it would happen right here in Ballynagowan."

Cillian nodded, understanding in his eyes. "Sometimes, the greatest adventures are the ones that happen in our own backyard. We just need to learn how to see them."

Maeve linked her arms through theirs, a mischievous glint in her eye. "Well, my friends, something tells me our adventures are far from over. Ballynagowan may look quiet, but who knows what mysteries are waiting to be uncovered?"

As they walked out of the park, Ruffio trotting happily beside them, Harvey couldn't help but feel a sense of excitement for what the future might hold. Ballynagowan had always been a town where the extraordinary lurked just beneath the surface of the ordinary. Now, as they stepped into this new chapter, Harvey felt a sense of certainty. Whatever challenges lay ahead, they would face them together. They were united as friends, bonded as a team, and committed as the guardians of their beloved, ever-mysterious home.

The street lamps flickered to life as they made their way toward O'Malley's, casting a warm glow on the cobblestone streets. In the distance, the old tech park – reborn as a cutting-edge scientific research facility – hummed with activity, its lights a beacon of progress and possibility.

Harvey breathed in the crisp evening air, filled with the scents of hearth fires and approaching winter. He felt a deep sense of contentment, of belonging. Ballynagowan had changed, yes, but its spirit remained the same. A place where magic and science intertwined, where history and future collided, and where ordinary people could do extraordinary things.

As they rounded the corner, the welcoming lights of O'Malley's Pub came into view. The sounds of laughter and music drifted out onto the street, a reminder of the vibrant community that had weathered the storm of the Quantiforge incident and emerged stronger for it.

Before they entered, Harvey paused and looked at his friends. He felt a surge of affection and gratitude.

"Thank you," he said simply. "For everything."

Maeve squeezed his hand while Cillian clapped him on the shoulder. No more words were needed; they understood.

The door of O'Malley's swung shut behind them, but the story of Ballynagowan and its unlikely heroes was far from over. In a town where the impossible became possible, there would always be new mysteries to solve, new wonders to discover, and new adventures to embark upon.

And Harvey, Maeve, Cillian, and Ruffio would be there, ready to unravel the next mystery Ballynagowan had in store for them.